The Body in the Lake

(Another Palmer & Pritchard Adventure)

By

Mark Reasoner

Chapter I

Corey Palmer and Michelle Pritchard chained their bikes and packs to the posts just off the dirt road they'd pedaled up. Most kids came up to this cliff when they swam in Lake Cyrus.

The kids wore swimsuits and their packs held towels and dry clothes for the ride back to town.

Corey stripped off his tee-shirt while Michelle removed her shorts. As he began moving down the trail toward the lake, he said, "Last one in's a ..."

"Stop it, Corey," Michelle said as she finished putting her shorts away. "Grow up. That joke is older than my dad."

Corey laughed at his friend and ran the rest of the way. He leapt off the cliff edge down toward the lake's cool water.

The two friends wanted one more swim in the lake before autumn settled over Wagner County and things cooled, and this Saturday was just perfect with the temperature in the high eighties and a cloudless sky. Even though they were almost a month back in school, it felt like summer vacation still.

As he worked his body into position to enter the cool water, Corey's instincts told him something was very wrong. He looked down, expecting to see the lake's clear water, but saw only darkness.

Corey tried to scream but the sound was cut short when he landed with a splat in the soft mud. He rolled over himself several times down the slope.

Up on the cliff, Michelle looked down at her friend and began laughing.

"How's the water, Corey?" she asked between giggles.

Corey stood up, shaking mud and muck from his hands. His filthy look and encrusted hair made Michelle laugh harder from above.

"Hey, where's the lake?" he asked, spreading his arms.

"Drained away," Michelle answered. "Duh!"

"But they weren't supposed to do that 'til next month."

Lake Cyrus sat behind a concrete and earth dam where Jewel Creek and the Choctaw River flowed into the Holanattchee River. The Army Corps of Engineers were scheduled to open the dam and draining the lake in early October to repair the structure and clean up the lake bottom. For some reason, though, they'd done it early and now the place was nothing but a mud bog between three hills.

Corey looked around. He saw mostly more mud, but there were tree stumps, boulders, what looked like old oil drums, and lots of other things he couldn't identify. He stood precariously on the slope, looking down a very long way to what was usually the lake's bottom.

He looked back up at Michelle. "It's really kind of cool. Come on down."

"No way," she said. "It's a mess and I'll end up looking like you."

"So what?" Corey replied. "We brought dry clothes anyway. We'll just have to find a way to clean up." He looked to his right.

"Hey, I think that's an old bike down there."

Michelle looked where he pointed. "I think you're right. I wonder how it got there."

"Let's check it out," Corey said.

Michelle climbed down the cliff and gently stepped into the mud. Her foot sank into the muck.

"Yuck. At least we aren't wearing shoes." She slowly worked her way down to where Corey waited.

"Don't even think about it, Corey Palmer," she said sharply, seeing the smirk on her friend's face.

"Busted," Corey laughed. He'd have to be sneakier to get Michelle as muddy as he was.

He could have just grabbed her and thrown her down. He was big enough, having sprouted four inches in the last year. Now he towered over his friend by half a foot. But Corey wouldn't do that. He liked Michelle too much to be that mean.

Michelle was still short and slight for thirteen, though she was filling out noticeably in her one-piece suit. She'd wanted to wear a two-piece suit, but her mother scotched that idea. Marybelle Pritchard worried as much about her daughter showing too much skin as she did about sunburn.

They carefully stepped down to the twisted and rusted bicycle remains. The front wheel was twisted several ways and the rear was half buried in the lake bottom. Most of the paint was rusted over.

"I think I know whose bike this is," Corey said. "Do you remember hearing about Wayne Heckman launching his bike off the cliff? I bet this is his."

"I remember hearing he broke his leg doing it," Michelle said. "It's why they put the bike rack back there and banned riding on the trails."

They looked around some more and kept walking. The hillside sloped sharply, so every step they took toward what was usually the lake's center took them further down. Soon they couldn't see the cliff where Corey jumped off.

Corey kept looking and talking about what he saw. Mostly old tree stumps and fallen logs, sodden from being underwater so long. But also a lot of trash, including many empty bottles and cans.

"I wish people wouldn't throw their trash overboard," he said.

"Me too," Michelle said. "It's no wonder they need to clean up the lake bottom. We need to take better care of this."

"I'm with you," Corey said.

As they walked across the mud, Corey's toe kicked something hard. He stumbled, almost falling.

"Ouch," he said, looking down for what caused his pain. He saw a piece of metal and bent down to pick it up. He wiped most of the mud off the thing onto his trunks, even though they were already well coated.

"Hey Shel, look at this." He held the object up. It was a big silver ring with a large dark blue stone. He felt a lot of decoration and symbols around the stone and down the sides, though couldn't make anything out through the mud.

"What is it?" Michelle asked.

"Looks like somebody's ring. I wonder if it's worth anything."

Michelle looked at the ring in Corey's hand.

"I wonder who it belongs to."

"Me, now."

"Oh come on, Corey," Michelle said. "It might really be somebody's and we ought to try and return it."

"I know," Corey said, putting the ring in his pocket. "But if we can't find who it really belongs to, I'm going to keep it. I think it will look good once I clean it up."

They continued on. Trees were present up on the old lake shore, but they saw only mud beginning where the water used to be. Soon they could only see dark walls of soaked earth all around them.

"I never knew the lake was this deep," Michelle said.

"Me neither," Corey replied. "It's no wonder all this stuff was never hauled out. No one could see the bottom when there's water."

He stopped and pointed down.

"What's that?" He pointed at something larger than anything else they'd seen. It was a faded light blue mostly rectangular shape facing them. One end tapered to a point.

"I don't know," Michelle said. "Are you going to check it out?"

"Sure. Let's go." Moving carefully but steadily, they went down the hill closer to the thing. Its shape became clearer as they approached.

"I think it's an old boat," Corey said.

They moved on down toward the large whatever.

"It's an old rowboat," Michelle said as they came to it. The boat lay mostly upside down in the mud, its blue marine paint now faded from being submerged for some time.

"I wonder how long it's been here," Corey said. He moved around the stern and crouched down to look underneath. Michelle followed and leaned over his shoulder.

"I can't see much, but there's a chain attached to the bottom."

"Is there a hole in the bottom?" Michelle asked.

"I don't see one," Corey said, "but maybe the chain is attached to something."

He reached in and pulled. The chain came free from the muck. Corey pulled harder, trying to find what the other end was attached to. Whatever was on the other end was almost directly underneath the two friends. Corey reached into the mud to see if he could grab what was held by the chain. His hand wrapped around something thin and cloth-covered.

He pulled one end of the object free, though it wasn't hooked to the chain.

Corey held a shirt-sleeve covered human arm.

"Holy crap!" Corey said, trying to stand. "It's an arm."

Michelle screamed and Corey dropped the arm, jumping up and back.

As they were standing down from the boat and the body, Corey lost his footing and fell backward into Michelle. They both landed in the mud with Corey on top and slid several feet down the hillside.

He succeeded only in turning to face Michelle, driving her deeper into the mud.

"Get off me," Michelle cried, shoving Corey farther down the hillside. She stood first, but was now covered in mud like Corey.

"I do not believe this," she said. "We found another dead body! We're jinxed."

Corey stood and made his way back to where Michelle stood.

"We're not jinxed, Shel," he said. "We're just lucky.

"Or unlucky."

"I'm getting out of here," Michelle said, moving away from where they stood.

"Wait a minute," Corey said. "We have to tell someone. We have to report this."

"Why?"

"Because that's what we're supposed to do. We can get in trouble if we don't."

"Besides," Corey continued, "maybe someone can figure out who it is and what happened. Like we did with Phil Cooper."

"Seriously, Corey?" Michelle said. "Do you want to go through all that? I'm not getting grounded with you again."

"That won't happen," Corey replied. "We're not someplace we shouldn't be—"

"We're slogging around the bottom of a lake!" Michelle exclaimed, walking back to where Corey stood. "We're covered in mud and we've stumbled on a dead person that somebody didn't want found!"

"Well, I'm going to call the police," Corey said. "Someone needs to be told." He started climbing back up the hillside.

"How will you do that?" Michelle asked.

"My phone's in my backpack," Corey answered.

"And that's where?" Michelle continued. "We can't even see the cliff where you jumped in."

"I'll figure it out when I see the shoreline." Corey kept walking uphill. A minute later, he stopped and turned back.

"I can see the swimming beach and the picnic area, Shel," he said. "I can find our bikes from there."

"And what am I supposed to do in the meantime?"

"Stay there. We'll need to show people where the body is."

"Oh no you don't, Corey," Michelle said. "You're not stranding me down here with this thing." She began trudging up the slope.

"Now what?" she asked, joining her friend. "We can see the shore from here, but the boat is down there. How will we find it again?"

Corey looked around and thought for several seconds.

"I've got an idea," he said. "I know how we can mark it for later."

"Great. What do we do?" Michelle asked.

"We need some pieces of trash. Some things with colors," Corey said. "Then we'll tie them onto a limb and stick it here like a flag."

Corey quickly found a long tree branch lying on the lake bottom. He brought it back to the spot. Michelle found an old seat cushion cover from someone's boat and two plastic six-pack can holders. She pulled the plastic apart to make two long strands.

Corey emptied soggy and rotting foam from the cushion and used Michelle's plastic to tie the orange vinyl to one end of the limb. Then he stuck the other end into the mud as far as he could. The makeshift marker stood fairly straight.

"Okay, that should work," Corey said. "And we should be able to see it from shore."

They climbed on up to the sandy area usually reserved for swimmers and sunbathers. Beyond this was a large open area with picnic tables, charcoal grills, and restrooms. Corey and Michelle knew where their bikes were from here.

Back at their bikes, Corey unlocked everything while Michelle dug her phone out.

"I thought you didn't want to call anyone," Corey said.

"I might as well," Michelle said. "We're both in this."

She didn't dial 9-1-1, but the regular sheriff's department number.

"Wagner County Sheriff's office," a voice replied. "How can I help you?"

"My friend and I just found a dead body in Lake Cyrus," Michelle said. "We need to tell the sheriff, police, the coroner, and whoever."

"Okay, slow down," Officer Brenda Shelton replied. She wasn't a deputy, but a Craigsville police officer. The city and county shared functions to save money, including night and weekend dispatch. Officers and deputies rotated to cover.

"Let's start with your name and exactly where you are."

"My name is Michelle Pritchard, and Corey Palmer and I just discovered a dead body at the bottom of the lake."

Officer Shelton recognized the names. She'd been part of Corey and Michelle's adventure in the courthouse clock tower just over a year ago.

"Okay, Michelle," the officer said. "Calm down and tell me everything. You know how this works."

Michelle exhaled. "Like I said, Corey and I found a dead body."

"How did you get down to the bottom?"

"There's no water. We walked down."

Officer Shelton remembered hearing the lake was being drained this fall.

"Okay," she said. "Give me some details. Exactly where did you find this body?"

"We jumped in off the cliff east of the picnic beach and went down the slope. We were looking at the junk all around and saw an old boat. The body was underneath."

Corey heard Michelle and spoke up. "Tell them it was wrapped in a chain attached to the bottom of the boat."

Michelle told the officer.

"Alright," Shelton said, "where exactly are you now?"

"We're at our bikes but we're going back to the picnic beach," Michelle said.

"Can you see this boat from there?"

"No, but we put a marker down the slope to show you where to go."

"That's great, Michelle. Just sit tight and I'll get people out there quickly."

After hanging up, Shelton called Sheriff Wingate, Dr. Driscoll, the medical examiner, and her boss, Chief Blaise. Lake Cyrus was county jurisdiction, but the city police might need to help. Then she dispatched the nearest units to the lake to secure the scene.

Chapter II

Sheriff Abe Wingate crossed his arms and looked sternly at the two mud-covered kids sitting on a picnic table.

"What is it with you two?" he said. "Every time there's a call with your names attached, there's a dead body."

"It only happened once before," Corey said.

"And that was still too many," Wingate replied. The kids looked down.

Activity swirled around, both on the shore and down in the lake. Three other sheriff's department cars were parked on the grass and the Craigsville Volunteer Fire Department brought their rescue engine and a grass fire rig to the scene. The medical examiner, Dr. Driscoll, and her techs brought an equipment-filled SUV to process the scene. Everyone also brought rubber boots or fishing waders to deal with the mud. Right now, most everyone was down at the body.

"We can talk about that later," the sheriff said. "Right now, I need your statements. What were you doing here, and how in the world did you stumble on another dead body?"

His radio crackled, "Sheriff Wingate."

"Wingate here," he replied.

"Abe, this is Mo Driscoll. Can you come down here? You'll want to see this."

"On my way," he said.

He turned away from Corey and Michelle. "Roscoe," he called to a deputy, "come over here."

"Get statements from these two and send them home," Wingate continued when the officer joined them. "Just get the short version. We'll get their full statements next week."

"You two will go straight home," he said to the kids. "And you'll tell your folks exactly what happened, because I will check.

"I'll also text you with a time to come by the office."

He started moving away.

"Do we have to go like this?" Corey asked. "Can't we at least clean up?"

Wingate stopped. He looked at the assembled equipment.

"Hey, Garland," he called to the firefighter standing by the grass fire truck. "Do you have water in that thing?"

"Of course," the firefighter replied. "We always keep it filled, even if we don't need it."

"Good," Wingate said. "Hose these two off, will you?"

After giving basic statements to the deputy, Corey and Michelle got off the table and went to the grass fire truck. Garland already had the hose turned on when they got there.

"This is probably going to be cold," he said, "but it won't last long."

He was right. Corey and Michelle were both shivering when the shower finished. Afterward, they took their packs and went to the restrooms to towel off and change into their dry clothes.

Sheriff Wingate opened his trunk to get his rubber boots. As he pulled them on, another car pulled in and parked right next to him. Rich Geltsin got out of the vehicle.

"Hi, Sheriff," the editor of the *Record / Times* said. "I hear you've got a body. What's the story?"

"How did you hear about this?" Wingate said. "We've only known about it for an hour or so."

"My old scanner still works," Geltsin replied. "I heard you dispatch everyone out here. So what have you got?"

"I don't know anything yet," Wingate said, "and won't have a statement until I do."

"That's okay," Geltsin replied. "I can wait. Meantime, if you don't mind, I'll look around."

"I certainly do mind!" Wingate said sternly. "This is possibly a crime scene and I will not allow you to mess it up by traipsing around. Stay here."

"And why are you even here?" the sheriff continued. "Why didn't you send one of your people?"

"Because I called your department for confirmation and found out who called it in," Geltsin said. "I've got a soft spot for those two and figured whatever they've found ought to be interesting."

"Then go chase them someplace else. I sent them home." Wingate walked away toward the empty lake.

Geltsin wasn't easily discouraged, so he waited until the sheriff was across the sand to the muddy lake bottom. Then he started walking toward the people standing near the fire trucks. They might be able to answer some questions.

Corey and Michelle came out of the restrooms dried off and wearing cleaner clothes.

Seeing them, Geltsin called over. "Hey, you two, I thought the sheriff sent you home."

"He did," Corey said, "but we needed to clean up first."

"Well, that's a break for me," Geltsin replied. "So what's the story? What did you two find this time?"

"A dead body, chained to a rowboat," Michelle said. "And the boat was sunk."

Geltsin took out his pen and notebook. "Let's have the details. How'd you get down there?"

The kids told him how Corey jumped off the cliff and then how they were looking at things on the lake bottom when they came upon the boat and then the body. They also told Geltsin how they marked the slope to find the site again.

"Good thinking, Corey," the editor said. "Now, can you tell me anything about the body itself?"

"No," Michelle said. "We only saw the arm when Corey grabbed it."

"And it just looked like it had been down there for awhile," Corey said.

"Do you know how long ago?" Geltsin asked. The kids shook their heads.

"Is that it?"

Corey looked at Michelle. "Basically," he said. "After we found it, we called the sheriff and after everyone got here, he told us to go home."

"Then you better get going," the editor said, "but if you think of anything, let me know."

"We will," Michelle said. The kids grabbed the packs and started for their bikes.

Wingate made it down to the scene. Four other deputies and six firefighters were already there along with Dr. Driscoll and her two techs. When he arrived, they were closing the black body bag and carefully trying to place it into a long basket attached to a cable from up at the picnic area.

"Hi, Abe," Dr. Driscoll said as the sheriff came up. "I wanted to let you know this is definitely a crime scene." She moved to the boat's underside.

"We've gotten the body ready to send up, but I can already tell this is no accident."

"How so?" the sheriff asked.

"Come on down and I'll show you."

Wingate joined her and looked into the boat. He saw the large cavity where the body had been, and noticed a white splotch in the mud.

"What's that?" he asked.

"Plaster cast," Driscoll said. "I'm trying to get a face mold from the mud. There wasn't much left on the remains."

"But that's not what I want you to see," she continued. "The body was wrapped in this chain. Really wound tight."

She pointed to the boat's bottom. "And the chain was secured to the boat itself."

"Okay, I see that," Wingate said, "but what's it mean?"

"It means this was intentional." Driscoll said. "It means this boat and maybe this whole part of the lake bottom is a crime scene."

"Okay, it's potentially a crime scene," the sheriff said. "So do your thing."

"You'll approve?" Driscoll asked.

"Mo, you don't work for me," Wingate said. "You work for the coroner. Do what you have to do."

"My budget works for you," Driscoll replied. "And the overtime's going to be sky high before we get everything processed and back to town."

"Besides," she continued, "we'll be lucky to get done before dark, and I'm going to need some different equipment to haul this boat out of here."

"I'll approve the overtime," Wingate said. "But what else do you need?"

"A truck for starters," the medical examiner replied. "The rescue truck can take the body to the morgue and one of my team can go along and get things started there. But there isn't anything up top to haul this boat. Then I'm going to need a place to put the thing so I can work on it.

"And that's not all. Your folks know what they are doing, but the longer they're here, the longer there's less coverage across the county. I know the city police can cover some of this, but do you really want half your shift stuck down here?"

"I see your point," Wingate said, "What do you want to do?"

"I can call Birdie over in Morris. He can send his team and the truck. When they get here, I can release your people back to their regular duty."

"What about the fire guys?" Wingate asked.

"I'll use them as long as they can stay. They're helpful, but not really trained to process a scene unless it was a fire. All I really need from them is the winch and the drivers."

Wingate nodded his approval and Dr. Driscoll made the call. While waiting, the team finished bagging the body and winched it up the hillside. It was soon loaded into the squad and on its way to the county morgue. The sheriff walked up beside it.

Back at the picnic area, Wingate spotted Rich Geltsin nosing around, asking questions of anyone who'd talk. He also grabbed pictures where he could.

"Geltsin, you are getting in the way," the sheriff said. "Get out of here."

"Not a chance, sheriff," the editor replied. "This is a story and I am going to keep working it. Freedom of the press and all."

"This is an active crime scene," Wingate said. "I can arrest you for obstruction."

"Now, Abe, do you really want the hassle?"

The sheriff thought about this.

"Besides," Geltsin continued, "all you can really stop me from doing is getting close-up pictures. I'll get the details, one way or another.

"I'll put those two kids on it, if I need to."

"Okay, okay," Wingate said, "I'll give you the rundown tomorrow, after we've had time to get everything organized. Call me for a time."

"It has to be before two," Geltsin replied. "That's when we set the front page for Monday."

After walking down to Corey's marker for some long-range photos of the rowboat, Geltsin left. He had enough to get started, and the sheriff's statement with the details from Corey and Michelle should fill in most of the blanks.

Forty minutes after Dr. Driscoll's call, Stuart Byrd, known as "Birdie" to friends and colleagues, arrived with his crew of crime-scene techs and a flatbed truck borrowed from a Morris towing company.

Byrd and Dr. Driscoll helped each other whenever needed. The Morris County man handled evidence and crime scenes better than Driscoll, where she took more time with autopsies. A complicated case in either county usually meant the two examiners and their crews joined forces.

Byrd and his crew came down the slope wearing rubber boots and hauling several equipment cases.

"What's up, Mo?" Byrd said.

"Sorry you missed the body, Birdie, but we needed to get it stabilized and stored."

"No problem, kiddo, that's your gig anyway."

He set his gear down on the mud. "So what do you need?"

"I need the boat removed from the mud as intact as possible," Driscoll replied. "Plus all the trace evidence we can find, soil samples, and anything else you can think of."

"But let me show you the chain first." Driscoll took Byrd around to the boat's interior.

"See that?" she continued, pointing to the chain's connection on the boat's floor. "What does that tell you?"

Byrd looked at the chain and bolt for several seconds.

"Probably the same thing it tells you," he said. "This was no accident."

"Come on, Stuart," Driscoll said, "I need more than that."

"I'm not a detective, Mo," Byrd said, "and I'm not going to speculate. Let's gather the evidence and process the scene. Then we can see where it takes us."

They set to work. With the extra techs and the remaining firefighters, things went quickly and Dr. Driscoll's goal of finishing before sunset was met with an hour to spare. The last thing removed from the slope was Driscoll's plaster casting from where the body's face had imprinted. Before leaving, Driscoll instructed the remaining deputies and firefighters to rope off the entire area in case they needed to take another look at the scene.

The rowboat and all the evidence went to an empty bay in the city-county maintenance garage. The body went to cold storage in the morgue. After securing and logging everything, Driscoll and Byrd released everyone to go home. Over a quick bite the two examiners made plans to reconvene Monday. Driscoll would do the autopsy while Byrd began examining and processing all the other items.

Sheriff Wingate made good on his threat to call Corey and Michelle's parents. He was pleasantly surprised to hear both kids had filled their folks in on what happened. He wasn't so pleased to hear neither Mrs. Palmer nor the Pritchards were going to discipline either child.

"Yes, sheriff," Mrs. Palmer told him, "Corey told me everything. Maybe he shouldn't have gone all the way down there, but I don't think he did anything wrong."

"Wasn't it Michelle who called it in?" Mrs. Pritchard told the sheriff in her conversation. "Seems to me she and Corey did the right thing."

"And Corey's okay after all this," Annette told the sheriff, "He's doing fine, in case you are wondering."

"No, Michelle doesn't seem upset by this," Marybelle said. "If you're interested."

"Yes, I'll make sure they come over to your office after school on Monday," both mothers told Wingate.

Neither mother was pleased with the day's adventure, but couldn't find fault with anything the two friends did. Both were also happy their children didn't appear upset or adversely affected by finding another set of human remains.

Corey found the old ring in his swim shorts when he tossed his muddy clothes into the wash. In the uproar of finding the body and then all the activity with the sheriff, he'd forgotten about it. He rinsed most of the dirt and muck off, but there was still lots of grime hiding the ring's design.

***

Rich Geltsin spent Saturday evening doing research on Lake Cyrus's history. He showed up at Sheriff Wingate's office precisely at ten o'clock Sunday morning. At two that afternoon, he held his usual front-page editorial and design meeting for Monday's paper.

After church and Sunday dinner, Corey rode over to Michelle's house. Michelle and her dad were working in the garage.

Pete Pritchard sold his old restored pick-up when his daughter was born, but never lost his interest in classic cars. He'd taken a new job that spring, still driving a truck, but now doing local deliveries in Wagner and the surrounding counties. He wasn't gone more than one or two nights a week, and never consecutively.

So he had a lot more time at home. Marybelle kept him busy with home improvement projects, and there was always yard work, but Pete now had time to work on an old car if he wished.

He'd found his new project just a month ago when he saw a 1968 Ford Torino GT Coupe for sale by a farmer outside Tyrone. He paid less than a thousand for the old beater, and though it still ran well enough to make it back to Craigsville, that was about it. The thing needed a complete rebuilding.

He parked it in the garage and started taking it apart.

Corey left his bike in the driveway and walked in the garage.

Pete looked up from under the car's hood. "Hi, Corey, how are you doing?"

"Hi, Mr. Pritchard, hey Shel," Corey said.

'Hey, Corey," Michelle said, looking up from the workbench on the garage's wall.

"So what brings you over here?" Pete asked.

Corey pulled the heavy ring out of his pocket. "I know Michelle told you what happened to us yesterday, but there was something else. I wanted to show you something."

"What have you got there?" Pete took the ring from Corey and looked closely at it.

"I think it's an old class ring," he said. "It feels like one."

"That's what my mom said," Corey replied, "but she wasn't sure. We tried to clean it up, but didn't have anything to get the gunk off."

"If it's a ring, you could use jewelry cleaner," Michelle said. "My mom has some stuff, doesn't yours?"

"She uses a machine to clean her rings and stuff," Corey said, "and she was afraid this was too big and heavy."

"She's probably right," Pete said. "So let's see what we can do."

He walked to the workbench and looked over the chemicals and other solutions on the wall shelves.

"Shelly," he said to his daughter, "why don't you go get your mom's jewelry cleaner? We'll probably need it later to finish this.

"Right now, I think this will get us started." He pulled a bottle of oil and grease remover from the shelf.

Pete pulled on some rubber gloves and adjusted his safety goggles. Then he dabbed some solution onto a clean rag and started wiping the ring with it. Corey came up to watch.

"Put goggles on, Corey," Pete said. "This stuff is really bad if it splashes you."

Several swipes of the cleaner removed most of the muck, but the ring's metal was still dark and discolored. They couldn't tell what color anything was supposed to be.

Michelle came back in with another bottle.

"Mom says this should work whether the ring is gold or silver," she said.

"Okay, let's give it a shot," Pete replied. He took a clean rag and poured a bit of the different cleaner onto it.

"Either of you want to do the honors?" he asked the kids.

"Sure," Corey said, taking the rag from Michelle's dad. He began cleaning and shining the ring. A pale silver color appeared in no time with what turned out to be a dark blue gemstone set into the metal. Wrapped around the edge were letters, and along the wide part of each side Corey found two numbers above small shield devices. Then each side tapered down to the ring's narrower bottom.

Corey put the rag down and held the ring in the light.

"I see a one and a nine on this side," he said, as he turned the ring, "And a six and a five on the other side." He held it out to Michelle.

"There's writing along the top edge," she said, and started rotating it. "United States..."

"I can't read the rest."

Pete took the ring from his daughter and looked closely. He smiled at the two youngsters.

"Kids," he said, "I think you've found someone's Navy class ring. It says United States Naval Academy."

"And the numbers?" Corey asked.

"Class of sixty-five," Pete answered.

"And I'd bet there was something mounted on the stone," he continued. "There's a small hole in the stone's center."

He held the ring at an angle. "There's some engraving on the inside, but it's really small. Can't make it out in this light."

"Somebody's initials?" Michelle asked. Mr. Pritchard nodded.

"Do you think it's worth anything?" Corey asked.

"Corey!" Michelle exclaimed. "Don't be crude. It belongs to someone."

Pete laughed. "Shelly's right, Corey. It does belong to someone, and they're probably the only people who'd think it was worth anything."

"But how could we ever find out who it belongs to?" Corey asked as he put the ring back in his pocket.

Pete looked at the young man. "Come on, Corey. After what you two pulled off last summer with Phillip Cooper? I'd bet you could find that ring's owner in no time at all."

"Yeah, I suppose," Corey said.

"Well then," Pete said, "I'm glad we could help. But it's back to work on the car." He ducked back under the open hood and Michelle started working at the bench again.

"What are you doing?" Corey asked.

"Right now I'm cleaning things Dad takes off the engine," Michelle said. "But we're going to pull the heads next, right Daddy?"

"That's right," Pete said from the engine compartment. "Thing needs a complete ring job."

Corey moved over to the car's other side and looked into where Pete worked.

"What year is it?" he asked.

"Sixty-eight," both Pritchards replied.

"Cool," Corey said. "Two-eighty-nine?"

"Three-oh-two," Michelle said from the workbench. "The bigger version."

"You know about cars?" Pete asked.

"Mostly history," Corey said, "but I know those were Ford's main engines for a long time."

"Still are, young man," Pete said, "though they have metric names these days."

Corey stayed until dinner, helping take parts off the old Ford and cleaning them up. He went home needing another shower and change of clothes before his mother would let him sit down to eat.

Annette Palmer began thinking she needed to teach her son to do his own laundry if he continued coming home so filthy.

Then again, at least he was getting some good wear out of things before he outgrew them.

Having grown four inches in the past year, Corey was going through clothes almost as fast as Annette could buy them. He'd outgrown one complete wardrobe and was stretching a second. Fortunately for Annette's budget, a lot of teenagers in Craigsville grew like Corey and so the thrift shops in the area always had things Corey could wear. If he didn't like them, she thought, too bad. He'd outgrow them soon enough.

Chapter III

The *Craigsville Record/Times* arrived in people's mailboxes and driveways by sunrise Monday morning and the town started the week with Rich Geltsin's large headline and story.

Mystery Body Found in Lake Cyrus
By Richard Geltsin, Editor

The story took up most of the front page with two pictures of the rowboat and the body bag coming up the slope. Geltsin included everything he'd learned, crediting Corey and Michelle with the discovery and quoting both Sheriff Wingate and Dr. Driscoll. He also told why the lake was drained and summarized the Corps of Engineers work on the dam and the lake.

Charlie Clyde at WMCJ read the story in the studio while he waited to go on the air at seven.

This will be good to lead with, he thought His engineer gave him the cue to start in.

"Good morning everyone, and welcome to Monday. This is Charlie Clyde with you on WMCJ, Hit Country 106 FM, and I'll be filling in this morning while we try to figure out what happened to the raging lunatics."

WMCJ's regular morning show was called *Raging Lunacy,* hosted by "Lunatic Louie" and "Raging Rick." The two characters played a few songs, but mostly filled the morning with outrageous jokes, more outrageous rants on any subject, and offbeat conversations with a regular lineup of callers. They urged anyone offended by their comments to call in immediately so they could insult the listener directly. Few took advantage and most everyone in the four counties either laughed along or tuned out.

A week ago, however, the guys simply disappeared after their show. There had been no sightings, no calls, and no messages. As far as anyone knew, they'd vanished.

The station still had to fill the hours, so management juggled the lineup. Charlie left his usual afternoon slot to take the mornings, giving up his Saturday morning show in the process.

"It's going to be gorgeous in the four counties today. Partly cloudy with highs in the mid-eighties. Slight chance of rain this afternoon, though.

"News from Wagner County this morning. The Record/Times reports two youngsters discovered a dead body over the weekend at the bottom of Lake Cyrus. Don't worry, folks, there wasn't any water. As most of y'all know, the Army Corps is draining the lake to work on the dam and clean things up.

"And also, as far as we know, it wasn't either of our missing characters.

"Interesting thing, though, the kids who discovered the body are the same two who found those remains up in the Wagner County clock tower last summer.

"Don't know much more than what I've read, but we'll try to bring you more as we learn it. For now, let's get started with an old classic from the great Conway Twitty."

At Craigsville Middle School, Corey and Michelle faced a lot of questions from friends and acquaintances. Most wanted details about how they found the body, but a few wanted to know how gruesome the remains were.

"Did you actually touch it?" Tim Crane asked Corey.

"Just the arm," Corey replied, "but that was enough."

"Was it murder?" Paula Terrill asked.

"We don't know," Michelle said. "After the sheriff and everyone got there, we had to stay away."

And so it went until class started.

As the bell rang to begin third period, everyone in Mrs. Hollis's English class grew very still. Mrs. Hollis was known as the strictest teacher in school, and always insisted her students be quiet and ready for the day's lesson when the bell sounded.

As she began speaking, Corey's phone buzzed. Mrs. Hollis stopped talking and no one made a sound. Two seconds later, Corey's phone buzzed again. Though he tried hard not to react, Mrs. Hollis homed in on him. As she walked to his desk, Corey quickly took his phone out to turn it off, glancing at the message as he did.

To: C. Palmer / M. Pritchard
From: Wagner County Sheriff

My office 3:30PM
AW

"Mr. Palmer," Mrs. Hollis said, "your phone. You know the rules."

School policy said no texting or messaging during classes. The penalty was having the phone confiscated for the rest of the day.

"But it's official business," Corey said. "The message was from the sheriff's office."

"And why would the sheriff be texting you, young man?" Mrs. Hollis said. "What have you done?"

This made several students chuckle.

"Nothing wrong, ma'am," Corey said. "It's about what I found over the weekend."

"And what did you find that would interest Sheriff Wingate?"

Now some of the others laughed louder.

"That's enough, people!" Mrs. Hollis said.

Tim Crane spoke up. "Didn't you read the paper, this morning, Mrs. Hollis?"

"No, I did not. I have better things to do with my morning free time than waste it on that silly thing."

All the students laughed.

"Am I missing something?" Mrs. Hollis asked. Corey mumbled a reply.

"What was that, Mr. Palmer?"

"Michelle Pritchard and I found a dead body in the lake," Corey said. "And the sheriff wants full statements from us after school. That's what the message was about."

"Well then, the sheriff will just have to get along without your information." Mrs. Hollis turned to go back to her desk.

"But you can't do that!" Corey said. "I have to reply."

Mrs. Palmer turned around. "No you do not. And if you aren't careful, young man, you'll be serving detention this afternoon."

"You're interfering with an investigation," Corey said. Several classmates chuckled.

"And you're insubordinate, Mr. Palmer." Mrs. Hollis replied. "You will serve two hours detention this afternoon." She wrote up a form on her desk.

"And if you say another word, I will send you to the principal's office where you can explain why you violated school policy and talked back to me."

"It's not fair," Corey said quietly, trying not to be heard. "I'm just trying to help out."

But Mrs. Hollis did hear him.

"That's it," she said. She went to the classroom door, and called to the security officer in the hall.

"Escort Mr. Palmer to the office," she told the man when he entered the room. "Tell Mr. Dorsey that Corey violated school policy and was insubordinate. Also tell him I've already imposed a two-hour detention."

Corey grabbed his backpack and left with the officer.

As they walked to the office, the man told Corey, "I don't know what happened, but everybody knows you don't cross Mrs. Hollis. I hope you aren't in too much trouble, kid."

Corey waited outside while the security guard talked to the principal. After the man left, Mr. Dorsey made Corey wait several more minutes before calling him in.

"Alright, Corey, tell me what happened," Dorsey said.

Corey quickly explained about the message from Sheriff Wingate, and then how Mrs. Hollis took his phone. When asked, he admitted he did talk back to his teacher, but tried to explain why it was important.

Dorsey stopped him. "All well and good, son, but you know the rules and you did violate them. Why didn't you turn your phone completely off?"

"I thought I had," Corey said. "And if Mrs. Hollis would've read the message, she might have seen I was telling the truth."

"That's not the issue, Corey," Dorsey said, "you did break the rules and you should never talk back to your teacher."

"I know, sir," Corey said, "and I am sorry. But I really do have to talk to the sheriff this afternoon."

The principal thought it over for a few seconds. "Alright, here's what we'll do. You go back outside and wait. I'll call the sheriff's office and confirm your story. I'll also let him know you'll be late.

"If everything checks out, you'll still have to serve detention, but that will be the end of it."

"Can I get my phone back?"

"At the end of the day, like usual."

Corey left the office. Ten minutes later, Mr. Dorsey called him back in.

"Well, son," he said, "Sheriff Wingate confirms your story, and told me how you and Miss Pritchard found another body. Seems to be a habit with you two."

Corey looked down.

"Don't worry. The sheriff said to come by whenever you're free."

"Yessir."

"And I called you mother too," Dorsey continued. Corey looked up with panic.

"What did she say?"

"I didn't talk to her. I talked to Judge Danielson, who said he'd pass the message along."

Dorsey stood and came around the desk.

"Look, Corey," he said as he walked the young man to the door, "the rules are there for a reason. Our gadgets can be a big help or a bigger distraction. Be sure you turn your phone all the way off before class starts. It's not that hard."

"Yessir, I know."

"Okay, now get going," Dorsey said. "And you caught a break. Mr. Holcomb's in charge of detention today. You might get out early."

Corey didn't see Michelle until science class later in the day. They only had two classes together this year, social studies and science. She'd already heard about his run-in with Mrs. Hollis.

"What were you thinking?" she asked him.

"I really thought my phone was off," Corey said. "Now I have to serve detention, and then go talk to the sheriff."

"And then tell my mom after I finally get home," he continued.

"Man, it stinks to be you," Tim Crane said as the kids entered class.

Teachers at Craigsville Middle School rotated supervising the after-school detention study hall. While there were basic rules, some set different standards, allowing students to use gadgets or read non-school books or something. The only things in common were no talking and homework had to be completed first.

Jake Holcomb taught seventh and eighth-grade math. He loved his job and enjoyed his students, but hated one modern development. Mr. Holcomb truly believed young people relied way too much on technology to solve math problems.

So he insisted his students be able to solve basic problems with just pencil and paper.

"However," he told every class, "you can also use the most powerful computer going—your brain."

When supervising detention hall, Mr. Holcomb made everyone finish their homework as quickly as possible, then he made them empty their pockets and put their packs and book bags at the back of the room.

After this, he put a problem on the chalkboard and let all his detainees work to solve it using only pencil, paper, and brainpower.

If solved correctly, students were released for the day with proper paperwork and allowed to go home early.

Holcomb put the day's problem up just after four o'clock, halfway through the two-hour detention. Corey wanted to get away quickly, so he went right to work on it, solving it within ten minutes. He turned his work into Mr. Holcomb and when his answer checked out, Corey grabbed his release and his backpack, and took off.

He almost made it out of the building.

"What are you doing, Mr. Palmer?" Corey heard Mrs. Hollis say from down the hall. "You are supposed to be serving detention. Where do you think you're going?"

Corey turned around. "I was released early, Mrs. Hollis—"

"That's not possible, young man," Mrs. Hollis interrupted, "I'm taking you back there right now."

"But—"

"But nothing, Mr. Palmer, two hours detention means two hours. Not a minute less. Let's go."

She escorted Corey back to Mr. Holcomb's room. As they approached, three other students left and headed for the door. Mrs. Hollis stormed into the detention study hall.

"What is the meaning of this, Mr. Holcomb? Why are students leaving detention early?"

"Because I released them," Holcomb replied. "They've completed their punishment and satisfied my requirements. Is there a problem?"

"Did you release Mr. Palmer here?"

"He was the first one done," Mr. Holcomb said. "Corey, didn't you show Mrs. Hollis your release form?"

"She didn't let me," Corey said.

"Don't worry about it, Corey," Holcomb replied, "you're good to go."

He turned to his colleague. "In fact, we shouldn't keep Mr. Palmer any longer as I know he's already late for another appointment."

"This is not acceptable, Mr. Holcomb," Mrs. Hollis said, "I will report this to the principal."

"Go ahead," Holcomb said, "but we both know Mr. Dorsey lets every teacher oversee detention as they see fit, provided the basic rules are followed."

"We shall see, sir," Mrs. Hollis said. "At any rate, I was coming down to return Corey's phone." She took the smart phone from her large handbag and set it on the desk. Then she turned and stalked out of the room.

"Are you going to get in trouble with Mr. Dorsey?" Corey asked as he pocketed his phone.

"No way," Mr. Holcomb said. "The principal does let every teacher supervise detention as they want. Within limits of course."

"Now get going," he continued. "You're already late."

Chapter IV

While Corey's Monday went south, Dr. Maureen Driscoll and her Morris colleague, Dr. Stuart Byrd, saw their day start off like most others and not change much. For Dr. Driscoll, the highlight was the call she received as she began getting ready to autopsy the body.

"Driscoll," she said, answering the phone.

"How come you get all the good ones?" the voice on the other end said without greeting. "And why'd you call Birdie to help instead of me?"

Driscoll smiled. She easily recognized the Cherokee County examiner, Gerry Peterson.

"It's simple, Gerry," she said, deciding to answer with her own sarcasm. "First, he's closer; second, I knew he could come up with the truck needed to haul the boat out of there…

"And third," she finished, "he doesn't whine nearly as much."

"Aw, Mo," Peterson said, "you've hurt my feelings."

Both examiners laughed.

"Okay, seriously, Gerry," Driscoll continued, "what's up? Do you want to help?"

"I'd love to, kid, but I've got a full house up here. Two accident victims and an old guy who likely died of a heart attack. His family insists on a full autopsy."

"But I do want you to keep me in the loop," Peterson continued. "Like I said, you do seem to get the interesting ones.

"And, I've got a brand new GCMS setup just waiting for a tryout."

"I'll remember that, Gerry," Driscoll said, ending the call.

Driscoll laid out all the tools she thought she'd need, then opened the storage drawer to retrieve the remains. Normally, she'd have a tech help her place the body first on a gurney and then on the table, but her crew was over at the garage helping Dr. Byrd.

It took a few extra minutes, but soon the body bag was centered properly on the examining table. Driscoll began by carefully removing the clothes and other effects. She recorded her observations as she went.

"We've got an adult male dressed in working clothes, blue jeans, chambray shirt, and work boots. Nothing extraordinary and these probably won't tell anything about when the body was placed in the lake."

She bagged the clothing for further examination.

"Even the underwear is very basic, white boxer shorts."

Dr. Driscoll put the clothes aside and began visually examining the remains. Though some decomposition had occurred, much tissue still remained on the bones. The lake bottom's cold temperature kept most of the body intact. She'd be able to gather lots of tissue, organ, hair, and other samples for testing and comparison.

The doctor began examining the whole body.

"There are no apparent wounds on the body, nor any readily apparent scars, birthmarks, or other identifying features."

She walked around to the opposite side.

"Scratch that," she said, "There appears to be remnant of a tattoo on the upper left bicep."

She stopped recording and took a photograph of the arm. The shoulder bone was partially exposed, but there was enough skin and muscle to show a partial tattoo.

Then she examined the head in detail. Here, she found what she was looking for.

"There is evidence of severe blunt force trauma to the left side of the skull above and behind the ear. The bones are fractured and caved in. Injury appears to be serious enough to cause unconsciousness and maybe death."

After completing her exterior exam, Dr. Driscoll cut open the chest cavity. Most of the organs were intact enough to allow several samples. When she cut open the skull, she found little remaining brain tissue, but enough to prepare several slices for later examination.

As Dr. Driscoll examined the body, Dr. Byrd and his team examined the boat over in the garage. With so many other people around, along with the noise from other garage bays, Byrd didn't try to dictate running notes. Rather he stopped and documented everything he felt was important as he found it. Beyond examining the chain and its bolting to the boat, there wasn't much to do. Byrd took paint and metal samples, in hopes of determining the boat's age and maybe how long it was submerged. There were no identifying numbers anywhere on it.

Byrd ran his hands along the rim up toward the bow. His fingers curled beneath the metal lip.

"Hold on," he said, finding something. "What is this?" He asked a team member to carefully climb into the boat and look where his fingers were.

"It's a piece of metal," the tech said.

"Broken off, or attached?" Byrd asked.

"Looks to be attached."

Byrd and the tech carefully documented the find, then they cut away that portion of the bow. They looked closely at the discolored metal riveted to the underside of the rim. It was a small rectangle, now rusted, but appearing to have some letters and numbers stamped into it.

Byrd took some cleaning solution from his kit and swabbed the metal. It was letters and numbers, *H-61-003*.

"A serial number, perhaps," Dr. Byrd mused.

"Do you think the owner put it there, or the manufacturer?" his colleague asked.

"I don't know," Byrd replied, "but we'll pass it on to the county sheriff and they can research it."

There was nothing more Dr. Byrd felt he could do with the rowboat, so he told his team to wrap things up and get ready to go back to Morris. He began organizing his notes.

When he finished, he called Driscoll.

"Hey, Mo," he said, "how detailed do you need me to be in my report?"

"Just the basics for now, Birdie," Driscoll replied. "You can give me the details later and I'll merge them into my final version. Do you have anything interesting?"

"Not much of anything," Byrd said. "Paint samples, metal, and that chain is all there was. We already gave you the soil samples, so there wasn't anything else there."

"You didn't find anything at all?"

"Maybe. We found a metal ID tag under the lip at the bow. I've documented it and I'm sending it with everything. But listen, kid, you probably could have done this yourself and saved the county some money."

"Probably so, Birdie, but I don't mind. You and your team are a big help."

"It's just going to cost you dinner, though. How about the Majestic?"

"How about you lower your price?" Driscoll said, laughing at her colleague. "Remember what you said about the budget. Wagner's going to owe Morris enough for your consult. And besides, I could always take Gerry Peterson up on his offer."

"What offer?"

"A new Gas-Chromo Mass-Spec he's itching to try, and he's mad I didn't call him to help."

"Alright, you win," Byrd replied. "Make it Connor's, but I still get to order a steak."

"Deal," Driscoll said. "Will you send everything to me today?"

"It's on the way, and I'm headed home.

***

Corey made it to the sheriff's office just after four-thirty. He asked the desk officer to tell Sheriff Wingate he was here. He didn't see Michelle.

The deputy told Corey to go on back to Wingate's office.

Corey closed the door and sat down across from the sheriff.

"Okay, young man," Wingate said. "I just need you to tell me exactly what happened Saturday and how you found that body. You're not in trouble, but anything you remember might help."

"Yes, sir," Corey said. "Have you talked to my friend, Michelle?"

"She and I finished talking a half-hour ago. I think she went on home."

"Okay. Here's what happened. We went up to the lake to go swimming since the weather is still so hot. We didn't know they'd drained the lake already, so when I jumped in..."

Corey told the sheriff everything he remembered from the weekend, from landing in the mud and finding the old bicycle, to how they made it all the way down to the rowboat and then found the dead body.

Then he explained how they climbed back up the slope, placing the marker to locate the boat, and finally told the sheriff about getting back to their bikes and calling in.

He didn't mention telling everything to Rich Geltsin, but since the story was in that morning's paper, Corey figured the sheriff already knew about that.

"Alright, Corey," Wingate said, "I don't have any questions. Your story matches Michelle's and fits with everything we found later. All I need you to do is write it all down and then sign it for the file."

Wingate passed a pen and pad across the desk.

"You can sit out at any open desk," he said.

"Yes, sir," Corey said, getting up.

"One more thing," the sheriff said. "How'd you come up with that marker half-way down the slope?"

""I don't know," Corey replied. " We just figured we wouldn't be able to find the body again from up at the picnic beach. We put it there 'cause we could see both the rowboat and the beach."

"That was really smart," Wingate said. "I doubt we'd have found the body without it."

Corey took twenty minutes to finish writing out his story. Then he signed his name to the bottom and took it back into Wingate's office. The sheriff thanked him and said he could go home.

Riding his bike home, Corey wished this day was over. All he wanted was something to eat and a chance to take it easy. But he still had to face his mother.

Annette Palmer already knew about Corey's appointment with the sheriff, but his detention was another matter. This was not typical behavior for her son.

On the other hand, Judge Danielson confirmed Corey's story with Sheriff Wingate before telling Annette what happened. Wingate told the judge it was indeed his text message that caused the whole thing.

So she wasn't going to punish her son any further. She did want details, though, and asked Corey as they set the table for dinner.

"Honest, Mom," Corey told her, "I really thought my phone was off. And it was important, it was the sheriff.

"I guess I forgot to turn it off after charging it overnight."

"I know, Corey," Annette said, "I heard the story from Judge Danielson. But you do know the rules, so pay more attention next time."

"I will," Corey said. "I'm just glad Mr. Holcomb was in charge, so I could get out early." He told Annette about how he'd done the match problem quickly and then how Mrs. Hollis tried to put him back in detention.

Annette chuckled over Corey's extra run-in with authority.

"Am I grounded or anything for this?" Corey asked.

"I think you've had enough grief over it," Annette said. "Let's eat and relax."

Since he'd done his homework in detention, Corey could take it easy. He watched a little television with his mom and then went to bed.

As he got undressed, he pulled the old ring from his pocket. He hadn't even thought about it all day, but was too tired to start now.

I'll try to work on this thing tomorrow, he thought, laying it on the nightstand.

Chapter V

The next morning, Dr. Driscoll finished organizing all the samples and packaged them for transport to the state crime lab. Wagner County didn't have the resources to do all the tests the doctor wanted, so she wrote up a detailed request for what she'd like done with each. She included fabric pieces too.

Driscoll also prepared additional sets, one for herself to work on to the extent she could, one to be stored as back-up in case any results needed to be confirmed, and the third to send to her Colleague in Cherokee County.

Might as well take advantage of his new machine, she thought.

After finishing with the evidence, Driscoll started writing her preliminary report.

Before she finished, her phone rang. She picked it up.

"Good morning, Doc," she heard from the phone. "Rich Geltsin with the *Record/Times.* Have you got a minute for some questions?"

"Questions about what, Mr. Geltsin?"

"About the body found up at Lake Cyrus. And I've told you to call me Rich."

"Not when you're asking me as medical examiner, sir."

"Okay, okay. So do have any new details for me?"

"Details about what?"

"How about who the deceased was, or cause of death? Things like that?"

Dr. Driscoll paused before replying. "No, sir, I do not. It is an ongoing investigation, and I am not at liberty to comment. You should direct your inquiries—"

"I know," Geltsin interrupted, "call the sheriff's office. You know what, Mo? You are just no fun."

Driscoll laughed silently as she hung up. Fun wasn't the issue and Geltsin knew it. It was about procedure, and she did things properly. She knew the editor would get what he needed, but she would follow the rules and try to make him do the same.

Driscoll finished her report, adding Dr. Byrd's notes and observations, and printed several hard copies. She prepared a copy for Sheriff Wingate, put another into her own files, got a third ready to mail over to Morris for her colleague, and marked the fourth for Chief Blaise at the city police department.

She knew the Craigsville police and the county sheriff's office cooperated and traded files. Might as well start right.

Like she did most times when there were results to deliver, Driscoll dropped the files off on her way out to lunch. It saved a bit of hassle, but mostly it freed her from answering questions until after others actually read her report.

Since this was a county case, she didn't just drop the file off, but made sure someone physically took possession. Sergeant DuPree was at the front desk, so he received the file and took it into the sheriff.

"Medical examiner's report," he said.

Wingate looked up. "Good. Pass it to Bobby and Ed."

Wagner County had two full-time detectives; Bobby Harding and Ed Ruter. Since they worked different shifts, overlapping only in the afternoons, they couldn't be called partners. Friends and colleagues, definitely, and they always kept each other updated on current cases.

Ed Ruter was just coming on duty when Sergeant DuPree handed him the file.

"What do you have, Arly?" Ruter asked.

"Report on the body in the lake," DuPree said. "Should I make a copy for Bobby?"

"No, I'll get it. I want to read it first." He sat down and opened the file. There wasn't much, just the initial crime scene write-up and Dr. Driscoll's summary, along with Dr. Byrd's notes on the boat itself. Most everything else needed test results before there'd be new details. Ruter read the summary.

Summary

Subject is an adult Caucasian male, approximately 6' tall. Weight estimated at 190 lbs. based on chest dimensions, waist measurement, and skeletal structure. Most, but not all skin and muscle tissue still present due to decomposition and immersion in water for an undefined period. Medium brown hair cut short.

Subject dressed in jeans, chambray shirt, and laced work boots. Items removed for analysis, but their generic nature gives no initial indication of when the body was placed in Lake Cyrus.

There was remnant of a tattoo on the subject's left upper arm, but not enough for a full identification. Photos taken and ink and tissue sample drawn for further analysis.

Remaining internal organs showed no indication of disease or trauma, though the long immersion could have disguised or eliminated any trace. Remaining lung tissue completely saturated.

The only injury was a deep fracture of the left side of the subject's skull, likely due to a severe blow. Further analysis may determine the exact nature of the wound, including the cause.

While skin and tissue remained on much of the body, there was not enough remaining on the subject's face to determine his identity, nor enough on the fingertips for positive fingerprint identification. A mouth impression was taken and dental records requested.

A plaster cast of where the face lay in the mud was taken immediately after the body was removed from the site.

Samples of tissues, bone, and skin were prepared and sent to the state crime lab for complete analysis including age, DNA profiling, toxicology, etc. Results will be forwarded when available. Additional samples also sent to colleagues in Morris County and Cherokee County for further study.

Conclusion

Most likely cause of death is severe blunt-force trauma to the head. It is unknown whether the subject was directly killed by this, or if he drowned after becoming unconscious and then placed in the lake.

Ruter finished reading and added the report to his own slim file.

Then he made a copy for his colleague. They'd talk about it later, when Harding returned to the office at the end of his tour. For now, the file joined twelve other open investigations.

Over at the Craigsville police department, Dr. Driscoll's report lay on the unattended front desk. When Officer Brenda Shelton returned from lunch, she picked it up as she passed by. She looked at the label and immediately read through it after getting to her desk. When she finished, she took it into the chief's office.

"What do you have, Brenda?" Chief Blaise asked.

"The ME's report on that body in the lake."

"That's good. Just file it with our other open cases for now."

Shelton didn't move.

"Is there something else, Officer Shelton?" the chief asked.

"Um, yessir," Shelton replied. "I was wondering if you could assign it to me."

Blaise leaned back in his chair. "It's not even our case; the sheriff is just keeping us in the loop. There's nothing to assign."

"But I'd still like to look into it," Shelton said. "And I don't think the sheriff would turn down the extra help."

Blaise got up from his desk. He walked around to close the door and motioned Shelton to sit down.

"What's really going on, Brenda?" he asked. "Don't you have enough to do?"

"I was planning to do this on my own time, sir. I wouldn't let it get in the way of my regular duties."

"And, I've got a ton of vacation time coming," she continued.

"Alright then," Blaise said, "accepting that, why do you really want this?"

"Well sir, I took the initial call, so I feel like I've been involved from the start. I'd like to see it through to the end. And, it's got those two kids involved..."

"And they could stumble over something," Blaise said, chuckling. "They are curious."

"It's also another strange mystery," Shelton continued, "with a body being discovered after it was hidden for a long time."

"I don't think we really know that," Blaise said.

"You're right," Shelton replied, "and that makes in even more interesting."

"Okay, suppose I let you do this," the chief said, "how would you start?"

"I'd first want to know who the dead man was," Shelton said, "then I'd start looking for a reason he ended up in the lake."

"That's going to take a lot of digging, and a lot of time."

"I know, sir, but I'm willing to do it. And that's where I think I can really help. I don't think the sheriff's detectives could take the time."

Blaise thought for a few seconds. "Alright, you can have it, but only under a few conditions. First, like you said, don't let it get in the way of your regular job. Second, you have to get the detectives to sign off. I'll take care of the sheriff. Agreed?"

"Agreed," Shelton said, smiling. "I'll talk to Bobby and Ed tomorrow before I come on duty." She started to leave.

"One more thing," Blaise said. "What do you want to get out of this? You passed the sergeant's exam, and you're getting your stripes next year if I get it approved in the budget. Are you pushing for detective?"

"Maybe," Shelton said as she left. Blaise smiled.

He called Sheriff Wingate and told his colleague what Shelton wanted to do. The sheriff set the same requirements. Now it was up to the detectives.

***

Corey and Michelle ate lunch with their friends, Tim and Paula, and a few others. Corey always brought a sandwich and some fruit, but bought milk or juice at school. Michelle usually brought hers too, but occasionally bought lunch. Today, she had leftover chicken salad.

As they ate, the friends talked about Corey's misadventures from Monday and the body the two found on the weekend.

"I still don't believe you two found another one," Paula said.

"I know," Michelle said, "I think we're jinxed."

"I wonder what other kinds of bodies are buried around here," Tim said.

Corey stayed quiet, eating his food. When he finished, he took the big old ring out of his pocket.

"What's that?" Tim asked.

"Yeah, Palmer, what's that?" a voice behind Corey said. "Let's see it."

Before Corey could react, Tommy Cooper reached over and grabbed Corey's wrist, turning Corey around to face him.

"What've you got, Palmer? Something you stole from that body?" Tommy's friends laughed.

"Go away, Tommy," Michelle said. "It's none of your business."

"Shut up, you little bitch," Tommy said, "or I'll deal with you too." He pulled Corey up from the seat, twisting his wrist. Corey grimaced with pain, but kept his fist firmly closed.

Across the table, Tim Crane stood. "Leave us alone, Cooper," he said loudly.

Tommy looked over, and Corey used the distraction to transfer the ring to his left hand unseen. Then he held it behind his back, waggling it at Michelle. She saw it and took the ring from her friend. She quickly put it in her pants pocket.

Tommy twisted Corey's wrist harder. Corey yelped in pain and opened his now empty hand. Tommy shoved Corey back onto the bench hard.

"What did you do with it, Palmer?" Tommy asked.

"Do with what?" Corey answered, rubbing his wrist.

"Whatever it was you had. Now give it up or I'll take you apart piece by piece until I find it."

Corey stared at Tommy, saying nothing. Cooper's friends looked around at the others. One noticed Michelle smiling.

"Hey, Coop," he said, looking at Michelle. "I bet he slipped it to his partner here."

The teacher on duty, Mrs. Kramer, noticed the ruckus and worked her way over to the area. She wasn't quite there when Tommy stepped over and grabbed Michelle by the arm.

"This will be fun," Tommy sneered, dragging her to her feet.

"Take your hands off me, Tommy Cooper," Michelle said.

"Leave her alone," Corey said at the same time. Tommy's other cohort grabbed Corey to keep him from interfering.

"What's going on there?" Mrs. Kramer asked, getting close enough to see things.

Tommy paid no attention. "Better give me what I want, slut, 'cause I'll take it anyway, and enjoy searching everywhere to find it."

"You'd like that, wouldn't you?" Michelle said quavering. Then she saw the teacher approaching.

"Stop touching me, Tommy Cooper," she said loudly, "stop trying to get in my pants."

Hearing this, Mrs. Kramer moved faster and called out for the security officer at the door.

"Break it up, now!" she hollered. "Everyone stay where you are." She moved between Tommy and Michelle.

"Did I hear right, Mr. Cooper? Were you trying to touch Ms. Pritchard sexually?"

Tommy said nothing. Other students began crowding around.

"Everyone, go back to your seats," the teacher said firmly.

"Officer," she continued as the security guard came up. "Take Mr. Cooper to your office. Be sure he talks to no one. Then call Principal Dorsey and tell him what is going on."

She turned back to the group. "The rest of you will take seats along the wall. Separate yourselves and do not speak to each other.

"Ms. Pritchard, you will remain with me." Corey, Tim, Paula, and Tommy Cooper's friends moved away.

The bell rang ending lunch and the other students began leaving the cafeteria. Mr. Dorsey and two other teachers fought through the flow to join Michelle and Mrs. Kramer. After telling the new arrivals to keep watch over the other kids, Dorsey asked for a report.

"I was coming over to break up an altercation when Ms. Pritchard told Tommy Cooper to stop touching her," Mrs. Kramer said. "I separated the two and sent Mr. Cooper off with security."

"I see," Mr. Dorsey said. "First of all, are you alright, young lady? Do you need to see the nurse?"

"No, sir," Michelle said, "I'm okay. He didn't really touch me in that way."

"Then why did you say he did?" Mrs. Kramer asked.

"Yes, why?" Mr. Dorsey added. "That's a very serious accusation."

"I was trying to get him to stop hassling us," Michelle said, "and stop trying to steal something from Corey."

"And he *did* put his hands on me," she added, "even after I told him to stop."

"But did Mr. Cooper try to touch you inappropriately?" Mr. Dorsey asked.

"I guess not," Michelle said. "He didn't get that far."

"He did threaten to," Corey said.

"That may be," the principal said, "and we'll look into it. But now we have the other matter to deal with.

"Why did this begin in the first place?"

"What was he trying to steal?" Mrs. Kramer asked.

"This," Michelle said, pulling the old ring out of her pocket. Mr. Dorsey took it from her.

He told Michelle to remain with Mrs. Kramer while he questioned Corey and the others. Corey told him how Tommy Cooper and his friends tried to take the ring away from him and how he slipped it to Michelle in the confusion.

"Cooper called her names and threatened to take it from her anyway," Corey said. "I tried to stop him, but his buddies held me back. That's when she hollered about him trying to… You know.

"And he *was* trying to touch her."

"I see, young man," Mr. Dorsey said. "And this ring?"

"I found it up at Lake Cyrus when Michelle and I found that body."

"Perhaps you should leave it at home," Dorsey said, handing the ring to Corey.

"For now, though, stay put." Mr. Dorsey and the other teachers quickly talked to the rest of the group. Tim and Paula backed Corey and Michelle, but Tommy Cooper's friends tried to blame Corey for starting it."

"Tommy just wanted to look at it," Joey Halston said.

"Yeah, Palmer didn't have to be such a jerk about it," Mike Bates added.

"Did Mr. Cooper grab Mr. Palmer to get the item from him?"

Neither boy said anything.

"Did Mr. Cooper call Ms. Pritchard demeaning names?"

Again, the two were silent.

"Did he grab Ms. Pritchard?"

Silence once more.

"Alright then," the principal continued, "I believe I have the picture." He turned to Mrs. Kramer.

"Mrs. Kramer, escort Mr. Palmer and Ms. Pritchard to my office and then ask security to come down here. Tell them to bring these two back to my office as well. The rest of you are released back to your classes."

"What about Tommy Cooper?" Mrs. Kramer asked.

"He can stay in the security office for now. I will deal with him afterward."

Five minutes later, Corey and Michelle stood in front of Mr. Dorsey's desk.

"This is getting out of hand, you two," he told them. "Two days in a row. First one of you breaks the rules on phones, and now both of you are involved in a cafeteria disturbance, making a very serious allegation against another student, which turns out not to be true."

"But he did try to steal from me," Corey said.

"And he did call me terrible names and threaten me," Michelle said, "and he did grab me."

"Perhaps so," Dorsey said, "though I haven't talked to Mr. Cooper yet. If what you told me turns out to be true, he will face punishment."

"In the meantime," he continued, "I need to do something with you. While I don't believe either of you is at fault, and your friends did back up your stories, you were still involved.

"I'm going to have to send a report to your parents, and have them sign it. I'm sure they will discuss it with you."

Both kids stiffened, but stayed silent.

"Beyond that, Mr. Palmer, I think that will suffice for you.

"As for you, Ms. Pritchard, you've made a very serious false accusation against another student."

"No I didn't!" Michelle said. "Tommy Cooper said hateful things, threatened me and really *did* grab me."

"And he tried to steal from me," Corey said. "Michelle was just trying to help."

"But he didn't sexually assault you," Dorsey said. "That means you lied to Mrs. Kramer and to me. We can't have that either.

"So you will have to serve detention after school for three days, and the incident will become part of your permanent record."

"But that's not fair," Michelle said.

"I believe it is," Dorsey said. "Even something like this can't excuse lying and false accusations. That's almost as serious."

"Should I have just let him have it?" Corey asked.

"No, Corey," Dorsey answered, "you shouldn't. Mr. Cooper doesn't have the right to take from you.

"Nor does he have the right to threaten or demean you, Michelle. But at the same time, you two should have said what he actually did, not accusing him of something else for a quicker reaction."

"It's a tough choice," the principal continued, "but the truth is almost always the best."

He sat down. "I'm going to call your parents now, then deal with the others. Get back to class."

Neither spoke as they walked out of the office.

"I hope he gets suspended," Corey said as they walked down the empty hallway.

"Whatever," Michelle said. "It still stinks. It's not fair."

"I know," Corey said. "But maybe you'd get lucky and Mr. Holcomb will be in charge. You'll ace whatever problem he puts up."

Michelle didn't react.

"Come on, Shel," Corey continued, "it won't be that bad. At least you'll have a chance to get your homework done."

"It's three days, Corey," Michelle said. "And I've never had to serve detention before. Now this is going to be on my record.

"And you're skating. You're off scot-free."

Corey thought for a second.

"Okay," he said, "how about I do something to get in trouble, too? Then we'd both have to stay after."

"Don't be stupid," Michelle said.

Mike Bates and Joey Halston also received three days detention, mostly for lying to Mr. Dorsey. Their stories trying to blame Corey and Michelle didn't hold up.

Tommy Cooper was suspended for three days, and his parents had to talk with Mr. Dorsey before he was allowed to come back. He also got detention for a full week. He missed two tests during his days out and wasn't allowed to make them up, resulting in failing grades for both.

Chapter VI

Corey knew he still had to face his mother over the incident, and decided he might as well get it over with. He left school as usual and rode his bike into town to the courthouse. He went up to Judge Danielson's chambers, but Annette wasn't there.

The judge was in his office, so Corey knocked and asked where his mother was.

"Running errands, filing papers, whatever is needed," Judge Danielson replied. "Court's done for the day, and we had a busy one. Is there something I can help you with?"

"No, sir," Corey said, turning to leave. "I can wait for her."

"What's wrong, Corey? The judge asked. Corey said nothing.

"Come on, son," Danielson continued. "Maybe I can help. At least I can let you practice telling your mom."

Corey's mom, Annette Palmer, was Judge Danielson's chief clerk. As a single mother, she needed the flexibility working for the court allowed. She also appreciated her boss's influence on her young son. The judge was pretty much the biggest male presence in Corey's life.

Corey sat down and took a deep breath. "I got sent to the principal's office again," he began. "But I swear I didn't do anything wrong. It was all Tommy Cooper's fault."

Corey explained how Tommy tried to take the old ring away, and how he passed it off to Michelle. Then he told the judge how Michelle got Tommy in trouble by saying he was trying to touch her inappropriately. He hadn't really, Corey said, but it got the teacher's attention.

"And that's when things went nuts," Corey continued. "And now Michelle has to serve detention and I have to get Mom to sign a form that gets filed permanently."

He sighed. "All because that jerk, Cooper, wanted to take something from me and Michelle was just trying to help. It's not fair."

"Did you tell your principal all this?" Danielson asked.

"Yeah, but he said it didn't matter. He said Michelle shouldn't have lied that way."

"That's true, Corey, no one should tell that kind of lie. Michelle made a very serious accusation."

"But Tommy was really hurting her, and threatening her, and calling her names," Corey said.

"Maybe so, and I'm pretty sure he'll be punished for that," the judge replied. "Have some faith in the system."

"Actions do have consequences," Danielson continued, "and being truthful is most always best. Hopefully, Michelle can learn that."

"It's still not right," Corey said, "she gets three days for trying to help me, and I walk."

"Do you want to serve detention with her?" the judge asked.

"I offered."

Judge Danielson laughed. "That's very noble, young man, and I hope you always stand up for your friends. But it's also kind of silly."

"Yeah, that's what Michelle said."

Annette walked into the office. "Everything's taken care of, Judge, and if it's okay, I need to leave early. I need to get home so I can talk to my son."

Judge Danielson cocked his head to the right. Annette followed his movement and saw Corey sitting in the chair.

"Hi. Mom," he said.

Annette froze, speechless. After a few seconds, she regained composure.

"I'm sorry, sir, I hope he hasn't disturbed you."

"Not at all, Annette. We've just been talking about his latest situation at school."

"Honest, Mom," Corey said, "we didn't do anything wrong. It was all Tommy Cooper and his guys."

"Principal Dorsey told me all about it, Corey," Annette said. "But you still have a lot of explaining to do. Honestly—twice in one week. What's gotten into you?"

"Don't judge prematurely," Judge Danielson said. "Listen to his story first. That's what we do around here."

"Alright, sir," Annette said. "But let's go. Come on, Corey."

"I've got my bike," Corey said.

"Go straight home."

At home, Corey explained it all again to his mother, from Tommy Cooper's attempt to take the ring, to Michelle's telling Tommy to stop, and then their talk with Mr. Dorsey. He also told Annette he still didn't think it was fair that Michelle got punished.

'What did Judge Danielson tell you?" Annette asked.

"He said something about actions and consequences."

"And Mr. Dorsey told you and Michelle that lying isn't acceptable, right?"

"So did the judge."

"Then you need to learn the lesson, young man, and so does Michelle."

"I know, Mom," Corey said, "I just wish I could do something to help Shel."

"Just be her friend, Corey."

"One more thing," Annette continued. "I think you need to do something with that ring before it gets you in more trouble."

Corey agreed, but had no idea what to do about it. He'd think about it and talk to Michelle when he could. At least he'd put it away someplace safe for now.

***

Corey was right; Michelle was able to get all her homework done during the detention study hall. At least she'd have a free evening, even though it wouldn't be any fun. She also needed to tell her parents what happened.

As she put her bike away, Michelle realized she wouldn't get a break, either, as her dad was home too. He'd been on the road since early Monday, but back now until the next day.

I have to face it, she thought, as she entered the house.

"I'm home," she called.

"In here," he mother said from the kitchen. Michelle walked through the house.

Both her parents were seated at the kitchen table where they ate most meals. Pete looked refreshed after a shower and change of clothes. His travel bag sat against the wall, ready for the next morning.

Marybelle looked the same as Michelle remembered from the morning. Apparently she hadn't been home long, though long enough to drink most of a tall glass of iced tea. Pete also had a glass in front of him.

"Sit down, young lady," Marybelle said. "And start explaining. How in the world did you end up in the principal's office and serving three days detention?"

"It's not what you think," Michelle said. "I didn't start it and that jerk, Tommy Cooper, was grabbing me and trying to steal from me. I just wanted him to stop."

"By accusing him of trying to touch you where he shouldn't?" Marybelle asked.

"Wait a second," Pete said, "nobody told me that. Are you okay, little one?"

"I'm okay, Daddy," Michelle said, "and he didn't actually touch me like that. He stopped everything when I hollered and the teacher came over."

"But he did threaten and grab me," she continued.

"So how come you ended up in detention?" Pete asked.

"Mr. Dorsey said it was because I lied and falsely accused Tommy."

"He's right about that," Marybelle said.

"But Mom," Michelle said, "I had to do something. The jerk would have taken the ring from me. I just wanted him to stop.

"I was just trying to defend myself."

"Then why didn't you just say he was trying to steal from you?" Marybelle asked.

"I don't know," Michelle said after several seconds of silence. "I guess I thought it would get people's attention faster."

"I guess it did," Pete said.

"Yeah," Michelle said, "but it didn't work out too well."

"No, it didn't," Marybelle said. "And maybe that's the lesson. You shouldn't do things like this."

"Should I just let him reach into my pants and take something?" Michelle asked. "Should I just let him do what he wants?"

"Of course not, sweetheart," Pete said. "You have to defend yourself. You can't allow any boy—or girl, for that matter—to touch you anywhere you don't want."

"Your father's right," Marybelle said. "And don't worry; we will back you up if it ever does happen."

Pete nodded in agreement.

"But you can't just throw that accusation out there anytime you want," Marybelle continued. "It can really hurt someone if it's not true."

"And besides," Pete added, "if you holler it too many times, no one will believe you if it's ever the truth."

Michelle looked at her father. "What do you mean?"

"Don't you remember the story of *The Boy Who Cried Wolf*?" Pete asked.

Michelle nodded. "It's a dumb story."

"Maybe," Pete said, "but it applies. The point is when you need help, people have to believe you."

"Do you understand?" Marybelle asked.

"I think so," Michelle said.

"Good. Now unless you've got homework, let's all pitch in and get dinner ready."

"Will you sign the form Mr. Dorsey sent?" Michelle asked. "I need to turn it in tomorrow."

They signed, noting they'd discussed the matter.

Over dinner, Pete talked about his latest run. The fall leaves were beginning to turn, so his daytime driving between deliveries was a little less boring. Oh the other hand, there was more traffic in a lot of places since school was back in session.

"I've had to adjust some appointments," he said. "But no one seems unhappy."

Marybelle mentioned some new books at the library. None interested Michelle, but Pete thought he might check out a new novel.

"A story about a place-kicker?" he asked.

"Uh-huh, a retiring one. Or at least one being forced to retire," Marybelle said. "It looks like it would be an easy afternoon read, and I think it has some good football stories in it."

Michelle didn't say anything as they ate. As they cleaned up, Pete asked another question.

"By the way, what happened to Corey? Where was he during all this?"

"Tommy tried to steal the ring from him first," Michelle said, "but Corey passed it to me. He tried to stop Tommy from going after me, but two other guys held him back."

"Is he serving detention too?" Pete asked.

"No," Michelle said, "he offered."

"Good man," Pete said, laughing. "Always stand up for your friends."

"But it would be silly," he continued.

"That's what I told him," Michelle said.

Michelle served her days without incident, even with Tommy Cooper's friends serving detention at the same time. She didn't see Corey outside of the classes they shared and lunch until Friday afternoon when she got away from school at the usual time. They rode home together.

"I am so glad this week's over," she said as they pedaled.

"Me too," Corey replied. "I think I'll stay close to home this weekend."

"Good idea. I'm helping my dad with the old car. Come over and help, if you want."

***

The rest of the week was just as uneventful for Officer Shelton. She couldn't connect with either detective until late that Friday, but finally arranged to meet them as they switched off. Detective Harding agreed to hang around for a bit, though he insisted Shelton buy coffee and sandwiches for them.

As they finished eating, Shelton told them what she wanted to do.

"Not a chance," Detective Harding said. "We don't need help. And besides, you're not a detective."

Shelton was put off by the detective's attitude, but forged ahead.

"So what progress have you made?' she asked. "Have you identified the deceased yet? Do you have any leads?"

Neither man answered.

"That's what I thought," Shelton continued. "Seems like you could use a little help."

"Come on," Detective Ruter said, "We haven't gotten anything back from the ME or anyone else. There's nothing to work with yet."

"When will you have something?" Shelton asked.

"Who knows?" Ruter replied. "But we'll work on it when we do."

"And we're quite capable of handling it ourselves," Harding added. "We don't need your help."

"Hey, come on guys," Shelton said. "The chief and the sheriff both signed off. They said it's okay."

"They also said we had the final word." Harding said. "And I think you know what mine is."

He stood to leave.

"Thanks for the food."

Ruter shook his head as the other detective left. "Sorry about that. Bobby's a little possessive of our cases."

"How many open cases do you have? Shelton asked.

"Enough."

"So why not take some help?"

"Like I said earlier," Ruter said, "help with what?"

"I don't know," Shelton replied. "How about we figure that out once all the reports come back from the labs?"

"I can live with that".

"Great. I'll let Dr. Driscoll know to send copies of whatever she gets to me as well as you."

"Don't you trust us?" Ruter asked, smiling.

"Trust, but verify," Shelton said.

Ruter put down his coffee cup. "I need to ask. Why do you really want to work on this? What are you getting out of it?"

"Keeping busy, for one thing," Shelton said, "and it's interesting. Another old mystery to solve."

"You mean like that boy they found in the clock tower last year?"

"Uh-huh. And it's those same kids who found this body, too. So it's got to be interesting."

"Alright," Ruter said, getting up. "I'll get Bobby to cooperate. Let's stay in touch until things start coming in. Then we can meet again to come up with a plan."

Chapter VII

During the next few weeks, nothing changed for the detectives or Brenda Shelton. The body remained in the morgue, unclaimed and unidentified. Dr. Driscoll's only work on the mystery was to work with her plaster casting. She carefully removed all the mud and debris, trying to expose whatever features were preserved. When finished, she took photographs from every angle and sent them to the state lab.

Dr. Driscoll also sent the photos to a friend up at the state university. Her colleague did research in anthropology, trying to reconstruct how ancient animals and humans looked based on skeletal remains. When Dr. Lois Lindlay looked at the pictures, she immediately called Driscoll.

"What have you gotten hold of, Mo?" Lindlay asked after catching up with Dr. Driscoll.

"Just what it looks like, Lois," Driscoll replied, "a partially decomposed body. I'm trying to reconstruct the face."

"I might be able to do something with this," Lindlay said, "but it could take time. Are you on a deadline?"

Driscoll laughed. "Heavens no. The body was in Lake Cyrus for close to fifty years. I don't think a few more weeks will matter."

Dr. Lindlay laughed too. "Okay, girlfriend, I'll set my grad students loose on it. By the way, do you still have the skull?"

"Yes. Why?"

"Because if your face cast doesn't work, we can always go back to basics."

Autumn settled into Wager County. High temperatures dropped to the seventies and overnight lows started dipping into the fifties. Leaves changed colors covering much of the landscape with reds, yellows, oranges, and browns to go along with the always green pine trees.

Days became shorter too, and neither Mrs. Palmer nor the Pritchards wanted Corey and Michelle riding their bikes to school in the dark. So carpooling became the order of the day. It was that, or riding the bus, which meant an even earlier and darker start each day. Not to mention getting home later too.

Annette and Marybelle switched off taking the kids to school each day. Getting home was harder, though Pete picked them up whenever he was home between runs. Their friends, Tim and Paula, also provided rides when asked. Every now and then, Corey and Michelle ended up at the library or the courthouse after school.

It might have been different for Corey if he'd said yes when the basketball coach asked him to try out. Being taller than most boys in his class, the coach thought Corey could be a good addition to the eighth-grade team. But Corey turned him down. He just didn't like basketball. He never played it, and rarely watched it. He preferred football, though he was much too skinny to play effectively. He liked running too, but Craigsville Middle School didn't have a cross-country team.

Initial reports from the state crime lab came back by the end of September. They confirmed Dr. Driscoll's initial observations, while providing more details and some new facts. She read the first overall summary, looking for anything she'd missed about the body itself.

Summary of Findings
White male subject approximately 30 years old. Tissue analysis *(appendix A)* reveals water and dirt inside the lungs peri-mortem. Blunt force trauma likely incapacitated the subject, but death caused by drowning.

Decomposition indicates body was submerged for approximately 40 to 45 years. Estimated year of death between 1971 and 1976.

Effects
Clothing and personal effects consistent with early 1970s time. Fiber analysis *(appendix B)* indicates no specific origin or branding for clothing or shoes. Items generic in nature and likely available locally.

Analysis of tattoo ink sample indicates foreign origin. Specifics unknown. Age of same indicate tattoo was done approximately three to five years prior to death.

DNA Analysis
Exemplars created and complete profile compiled. *(appendix C)* Results sent for comparison to US Armed Forces, CODIS and state DNA database. Initial results negative—no matches. Further analysis and comparison will require additional requests.

Dr. Driscoll read the appendices next, but nothing stood out. She then read the second report. This contained the details on the boat, its paint, and the metal tag Dr. Byrd found. All it said was the boat was most likely about ten years older. It gave no clue about origin or ownership.

This would be something she'd have Gerry Peterson look at, giving him the chance to show off his new toy. She made a copy of the reports to send up to Cherokee County.

After calling her colleague to let him know new information was on the way, and telling Peterson what she was looking for, she made copies for the sheriff and city police. Now there was nothing to do but wait for something to develop.

The Army Corps of Engineers began the major work on Lake Cyrus in October, and the *Record / Times* produced a long detailed article about what was happening and when the county could expect things to be finished. As a sidebar, Rich Geltsin wrote an update on the body, asking the readers to tell the sheriff or the paper anything they might know. He asked Dr Driscoll for new details, but once again got nowhere. The sheriff's detectives weren't helpful either, but they did give Geltsin a few details, such as the official cause of death and the timeframe.

They also mentioned Officer Shelton's involvement. Geltsin called the officer, but she couldn't offer anything new either.

The next week, after reading the paper's new coverage, Shelton met with the detectives and asked for an update and a plan.

"There's just nothing here," Detective Harding told her. "And I doubt there will be until the medical examiner releases more details."

"If there are any," Detective Ruter added.

"But at least there's a time frame," Shelton said. "The death occurred forty to forty-five years ago. That's something."

"So what?" Harding said. "It's not like we can just Google deaths in Wagner County from nineteen seventy to seventy-five."

"There have to be records," Shelton said.

"There are," Ruter said, "but they're buried in the basement or in a warehouse. I'm not digging through all that stuff for god knows what."

"Besides, what would you look for?" Harding asked. "There wouldn't be a death notice, since the body was just found."

"Maybe a missing person," Shelton said. The two detectives thought about this.

"It's a possibility," Ruter said, "but it's still not enough. Where would we start?"

"We could start with that," Shelton said. "Start with any missing persons from those years."

"Oh come on," Harding said. "We've got open cases to work on, with more coming every day. When would we find time to crawl through all those old cases? And you've got your own job to do."

"Hold on, Bobby," Ruter said. "Officer Shelton wants to help, and she said she'd do it on her own time. Why don't we let her start with this?"

Aren't you going to help?" Shelton asked.

"Nope," Harding said. "This is all yours."

"We'll authorize you to go through the county files," Ruter added, "but that's it, unless you come up with something."

"Thanks a lot guys."

"Don't take it too hard, Brenda," Ruter said. "At least you'll only have one place to search. The city and county records are stored together."

"Keep us informed," Harding said, ending the meeting.

Shelton also needed her chief's okay to search the old records. Chief Blaise quickly said yes, but warned her of what to expect.

"I wish you luck," he said, "and I hope you know what you're getting into."

"What do you mean, sir?"

"You'll need to look through every box and file for all those years. Both city and county, and there's no organization at all."

"How many records are there?" Shelton asked.

"More than you think," the chief answered. "Everything from vandalism, to reports of prowlers, to stolen cars, and so on. We might be a small community, but there's still a lot happening."

"I'll just have to keep at it," Shelton said.

"There's an easier way, you know," Blaise said.

"What's that?"

"The paper. While we don't have an index, so to speak, the *Record / Times* always publishes all the police and sheriff's calls for each day. Why don't you check there first?"

Shelton smiled. A great idea, she thought, and she was sure Rich Geltsin would let her go through back issues. She thanked the chief and returned to her desk.

***

Corey read the paper's stories on the lake and the body he and Michelle found. They didn't tell him anything knew, but did remind him of their adventure. He wished there was something he could do to help find out who the dead person was, but couldn't figure out where to start.

His phone rang as he finished his homework one evening later that week. The caller ID showed Michelle's name and number.

"Hey, Shel," he said.

"Hi Corey, how's it going? Did you finish that math assignment?"

"Yeah, it was hard though."

"I know. What did you get for the last equation? I got x was seventeen."

"Me too." Neither spoke for a few seconds.

"Shel," Corey finally said, "did you read the paper's stories on the lake?"

"I glanced at them. What about them?"

"I was just wondering if there was something we could do?"

"You're kidding," Michelle said. "What in the world could we do?"

"I don't know," Corey said, "but I bet we could help, like we did with Philip Cooper."

"Don't be silly, Corey," Michelle replied. "Look at all the trouble we had when we dug into that story."

"I know. But it was fun, wasn't it?"

"I guess, but I don't really want to do it again. Besides, this time the police and sheriff are looking into it."

"Yeah, you're right," Corey said.

Still thinking about the body and how they found it, Corey remembered the old ring. He dug it out of his dresser.

"We can look into this," he told himself. "Nobody else knows where we found it, so we won't be in anyone's way.

He called Michelle. "Hey Shel," he said when she answered. "Remember that old ring we found?"

"What about it?"

"Let's try to find out who owned it."

"Why?"

"Like you said when we found it and when we showed it to your dad. It might be important to someone."

"Okay," Michelle said after a few seconds. "But where do we start?

"I don't know," Corey replied.

Well, it's a ring, so maybe we could have a jeweler look at it."

Corey brightened. His friend once again had a good idea.

"You're right, Shel," he said, "We could take it to that jewelry store out at the mall. I bet they could tell us something about it."

"Yeah, but they'd have to keep it for awhile, wouldn't they? And we wouldn't be able to research anything while they did."

Corey thought for a moment. "You're right. But we could take some pictures of it so we'd still have something to work with."

"Good idea. Will you email them to me?"

Corey agreed and hung up. Using his phone, he took pictures of the ring from every side, placing it on a blank piece of white paper as background. He tried to get as close up to the ring as he could, especially with the inside views. As he took these, he noticed some markings. One looked fairly distinct, but he couldn't make it out. On the other side he saw what looked like some faded letters.

He emailed the photos from his phone to himself and Michelle. From his computer, he printed off copies to take with him.

Marybelle entered Michelle's room as she opened the file from Corey to look at the pictures.

"What are you looking at?" she asked.

"Pictures from Corey," Michelle said. "That old ring he found in the lake."

"Are you going to try and find the owner?"

"Yes ma'am."

"Well, good luck, but don't forget your schoolwork." Marybelle left.

Looking at the pictures, Michelle began thinking about what it meant. The Naval Academy was a big deal, she knew, not like just going to any college. There probably weren't too many people from Craigsville or Wagner County who got accepted.

This might not be that hard, she thought as she closed the file and shut down her computer for the evening. She'd talk to Corey about it the next day.

Chapter VIII

Mr. Isaacs straightened the pile of social studies exam papers and looked out over his class.

"Alright folks," he said, "everyone's test is in, and that will do it for this week. We start a new unit on Monday, so no homework this weekend."

He paused while his students clapped. "Now I know we've still got twenty minutes until the bell, but I can't let you go early."

Two students in the back moaned, "Awww…" Everyone laughed.

"I know, I know," Mr. Isaacs said, joining the laughter. "But those are the rules. However, you can do what you want with the rest of the period, as long as you're quiet."

"Can we surf the web? One student asked.

"Sure," Isaacs replied, "within school guidelines."

"Can we sleep?" another student asked to more laughter.

"No snoring," Isaacs said.

Ron Isaacs tried to give his students this small break at the end of each unit throughout the semester. With all the regular class work, homework and tests, his social studies classes were as hard as anything the eighth-graders faced. So when one section of work was finished and tested, he liked to give the kids a short break. A little free time on a Friday afternoon and no weekend homework wasn't much, but no one complained.

"Mr. Isaacs?" Paula Terrill asked. "Can some of us talk about the dance? We're on the committee."

"Sure. Work in the back."

People began talking quietly, pulling out books and tablets, or just slouching in their seats. Paula's group of four moved to the back row, arranging desks in a square.

Mr. Isaac's seating arrangement had Corey and Michelle on the front row.

"I thought of something, Corey," Michelle said, as she brought her backpack up to the desktop. "It's about the ring."

She took the photos out and put her pack down. "This thing is from the Naval Academy, and that's a pretty big deal."

"Uh-huh," Corey said. "So what?"

"So it shouldn't be too hard to find out about someone who got in. There probably weren't too many."

"You're probably right," Corey said, "but it was a long time ago. The ring says nineteen sixty-five. How can we find someone from back then?"

"Yearbooks," Mr. Isaacs said. He might be giving the kids some free time and free rein, but he still paid attention. He came around his desk.

"Why don't you look at the old high school yearbooks? I'll bet there are notes about what colleges kids were headed off to."

"That's right," Michelle said, "and I'll bet the library has all the old ones, too. All we need to do is look in that year."

"Hold on, Michelle," Mr. Isaacs said. "You won't find what you're looking for in that volume."

"What do you mean?" Corey asked.

Isaacs took the picture showing the six and five on one side. "The date is the class year. It means the person graduated in sixty-five. So he would have entered four years earlier."

"Okay," Corey said, doing the quick calculation. "That means he graduated from high school in nineteen sixty-one."

"That's a good start, Corey," Isaacs said. "That's where you should look."

The bell rang and all the students began leaving. Michelle stuffed the printed photos into her pack and got up to leave with Corey.

"Hey, you two," Mr. Isaacs said. "Is this going to be your research project, trying to find the ring's owner and history?"

Corey and Michelle looked at each other.

"I don't know," Corey said. "We haven't talked about it."

"We'll have to see where it leads," Michelle said.

They left the classroom. Walking out of the building, they caught up with Tim Crane. His mother was giving them a ride.

"Want to hit the library tomorrow?" Michelle asked.

"I was going to ask my mom to take me out to the mall," Corey replied. "I wanted to let the jewelry store look at the ring."

"Cool," Tim said, joining the conversation. "Let's all go. I'll call Paula and Renee and we can meet at the food court."

"If our moms will take us," Corey said.

"And my mom has to work," Michelle said. "That's why I wanted to look at the yearbooks tomorrow. I won't be able to go anywhere."

"What yearbooks?" Tim asked. Corey explained what he and Michelle were going to look up and why.

"Okay," Tim said, "why don't we all meet at the library, and then we can figure out getting to the mall."

"I bet my mom will take all of us," Corey said.

Annette agreed to take the group on Saturday. She had shopping to do anyway. Corey texted all his friends setting the next day's arrangements and time.

"Does the library have the old high school yearbooks?" Michelle asked her mother as they cleaned up from dinner.

"Of course," Marybelle replied. "What are you looking for?"

Michelle explained what Mr. Isaacs told her earlier. "So we figured we could look up anyone from Wagner County who got accepted to the Naval Academy back then."

"Well, you could, but it's not that simple," Marybelle said. "You'd have to look through a lot of yearbooks, even with just one year."

"What do you mean, Mom?"

"Honey, Wagner County High School hasn't been around that long. It didn't exist in the year you want to look at.

"The school was consolidated in the seventies. Before that, there was Craigsville High, Indian Valley, Augusta, Tompkinsville, North Township, and Lee Township. And that's just around here."

"But wouldn't the library have the yearbooks from all those?" Michelle asked.

"I think so," Marybelle said. "At least we should have most of them. Lee Township is still independent, you know."

"But there are also the schools in the other counties," she continued, "and I don't think we have many of them. I can call the other libraries if you like."

"Thanks, but I'm wondering if this is such a good idea," Michelle said.

"It is a good idea," Marybelle said, "but you need some more information."

"What do you think we should do?"

"Why don't you go ahead and check the yearbooks we have. Who knows, you might find what you're looking for."

Michelle went to the library with her mom early the next morning. By the time Corey and the others showed up, she'd found all the nineteen sixty-one yearbooks for the old schools and set them on a table in the back. Everyone took a volume to look through.

"What are we looking for?" Renee asked.

"Someone set to go to the US Naval Academy," Corey said. "Check the senior class."

Tim had the easiest one. Augusta High School had less than two hundred students back then, and just thirty seniors. He looked through the entire book in less than ten minutes.

"Nothing here," he said, closing the old volume.

"Same with Tompkinsville," Paula said a couple of minutes later.

Corey finished North Township and Lee Township by the time Michelle finished looking through Indian Valley. Neither found any mention of a graduate being appointed to Annapolis.

Renee was still looking through Craigsville, and taking a lot of time. She turned the pages slowly, checking out each picture and caption.

"Come on," Corey said. "What's taking so long?"

Renee looked up. "I recognize a lot of names. I even think I know some of these people."

"Like who?" Tim asked.

Renee turned the book around and pointed to a picture. "That's your dad, isn't it?"

Tim looked at the picture. "Not my dad, my granddad."

"Who else have you found?" Michelle asked.

"I think the girl in the next picture is old Ms. Baxter."

Paula looked at the book. "I think you're right. But who's the other woman?"

"I don't know."

For the next twenty minutes, they all took turns looking at the Craigsville High yearbook. There was nothing about what college any of the seniors were headed to, but they still had fun picking out names they knew and trying to match these fifty-some-year-old pictures with the people they knew today.

Annette arrived at ten-thirty to pick them up. They set one-thirty to meet for the ride home. Inside the mall's main entrance, they began splitting up, as each friend came to where they wanted to start. They'd meet for lunch at the food court at noon.

Corey left the group first, heading into Jason's Jewels. He approached the counter where an older man was looking at some papers. Henry Jason owned and ran the store. A third-generation jeweler, he'd inherited the original store from his parents. The shop used to be in town, three blocks from the square, but Henry moved it to the mall to attract more customers from the surrounding counties.

"Can I help you, young man?" he asked, smiling.

"Um, yessir," Corey said. He took the ring out of his pocket. "I wanted to ask about this ring I found."

"Let's see," Mr. Jason said, taking the ring and turning it over in his hands. "An old class ring, probably silver, with a good size stone, but probably not a major gemstone. Not really worth much, son. I'm sorry." He put the ring down on the counter.

"I'm not looking for what it's worth," Corey said, "I'm trying to find out about it. I'd like to find who it belongs to."

"Okay, that's different," Mr. Jason said, picking the ring up again. He took a loupe from his pocket and examined the ring closely.

"Hmm," he continued. "There might be something here. Can you let me take a closer look?"

"I guess so," Corey said, "but how long would it take? I have to meet my friends later."

"Not that long," Mr. Jason said, "and you can watch if you want."

Corey smiled. "Great."

"Then come on back, Mr…"

"Corey Palmer."

"Nice to meet you. I'm Henry Jason." As Corey went around the counter, Mr. Jason asked his colleague to keep an eye on things for a few minutes.

In the back room, Jason sat down at his workbench and turned on a bright light. Then, he placed the ring onto a stand, clamping it in place so he could work with both hands.

"Alright, Corey," he said, "let's take a closer look." Jason peered through his glass.

"Have you checked the inside of the ring?"

"Yes, and I think there are some markings."

"You're right," Mr. Jason said, "Come here and see what you think."

Corey used the magnifying glass Mr. Jason offered and looked at the ring's inside. The one mark he'd seen earlier was now very clear. He saw letters stamped into the metal and made out *Herff.*

"Is this the owner's name?" he asked.

Mr. Jason laughed. "If it was, most every ring like this would belong to the same person.

"That's the maker's hallmark, Corey. Their signature, if you will. This ring was made by Herff-Jones & Company. Not surprising, as they make most class rings in the country. Have for years."

"Could they tell us who they made this one for?" Corey asked.

"Well, you could write to them and ask," Mr. Jason replied, "but I doubt they'd still have records from back then. I can give you an address and a contact, if you want."

"Thanks," Corey said.

"No problem. But keep looking, there is something else."

Corey looked at the ring again. "There are some marks on the other side."

"Yes there are," Mr. Jason said, "and those might be what you are looking for. I'm going to try and bring them out."

He took a bottle from the shelf above the workbench and a cotton swab. Dipping the swab in the bottle, he gently rubbed it over the ring's inside where they'd seen the other marks.

"This will sink into any engravings, giving us some contrast."

After several seconds, Mr. Jason looked through the magnifying glass again."

"I believe we have initials, Corey. I can make out a *P,* an *M,* and an *S.*"

"Could they be the owner's initials?" Corey asked.

"Most likely," Mr. Jason said. "If they aren't, they might be someone very close to the owner, like a fiancée or wife."

"Wow," Corey said. "Now we can look for someone with those initials."

"Yes you can," Mr. Jason said, giving the ring back. "And I'm glad I could help."

"Can I ask one more thing?" Corey said. "Do you know why there's a hole in the top?"

The jeweler looked at the very small hole in the stone.

"I can't say for sure," he said. "But I suspect it was some kind of insignia. Maybe an anchor, it's a Naval Academy ring, after all. I can look into it further if you want."

"That's okay," Corey replied. "This really helps. Thank you, Mr. Jason."

Corey left the store and went back into the mall.

The group gathered in the food court a few minutes before noon. Renee and Michelle each had small plastic bags from a clothing store and Tim had one from the large department store.

As they sat down to eat, Paula asked what the other girls bought.

"A new top," both answered, showing their purchases to the others.

"Did you get anything?" Michelle asked.

"I found a dress for the dance," Paula said, "but I need my mom to check it out and then buy it."

"Someone asked you to the dance?" Tim asked in a dramatic tone. Paula punched him in the shoulder.

"Yes and that someone needed to buy a real necktie," she said. "I'm not going with anybody wearing a stupid clip-on."

The others laughed.

"How about you guys?" Paula asked.

"I'll probably go," Renee said, "but no one's asked me yet. I doubt anyone will."

"No one's asked me," Michelle said, looking directly at Corey, who ate silently.

Tim waved his hand in front of Corey's face. "Earth to Corey, come in."

"Huh? What?" Corey said.

"We're talking about the dance," Paula said. "Are you going?"

"I don't know," Corey said. "I guess so."

Michelle stared harder.

"Sorry, I was thinking about something else," Corey continued. "I found some stuff out about that ring. We might be able to find the owner after all."

The others were silent. Corey took the ring from his pocket.

"There are some initials on the inside and a mark from the company who made it. Mr. Jason, the jeweler, even said he'd…"

"That's cool, man" Tim interrupted, "but it's not what we were talking about."

"We were asking if you were going to the dance," Paula said, "and if so, were you going to ask anyone."

"Um, I hadn't thought about it," Corey said. "Who would I ask?"

Michelle stood up, grabbed her sack and stalked off.

"You are totally clueless, aren't you Palmer?" Renee said, getting up to go after Michelle. Paula joined her, leaving the boys alone at the table."

"What was that about?" Corey asked Tim.

'I think you just blew it, dude," Tim answered. "I think Michelle was hoping you'd ask her."

"Oh," Corey said.

"You're going to, aren't you?"

"I don't know. I figured we'd just go and hang out together, but not like a date or anything."

"I don't think that's what she wants, Corey."

Only Tim and Corey met Annette at one-thirty to head home. As the boys got in the car, she asked where the girls were.

"Paula's meeting her mom to look at a dress," Tim said. "And Michelle got mad during lunch and went off. Renee's with her and they're getting a ride from one of their folks."

"What did Michelle get mad about?" Annette asked.

"Well," Tim answered, "I think she wanted Corey to…"

"Shut up, Tim!" Corey said sharply.

"It's nothing, Mom," he continued, "a misunderstanding."

No more was said on the drive home. Annette dropped the boys at the library so they could get their bikes.

When Corey got home, Annette met him in the kitchen.

"Do you want to talk about it?" she asked.

"No," Corey said, walking away toward his room.

Pete Pritchard picked the girls up from the mall. Renee's mother wasn't available and Marybelle was working at the library, so he got the job.

Paula joined them, too. After her mother joined them, they bought the new dress for the dance. Michelle and Renee found dresses they liked as well, though neither could buy one.

While Michelle sulked in the front seat, the other two girls chatted happily in the back. Pete knew better than to get in the middle of that conversation, so he just listened. He dropped the others at the library for their bikes and drove home with Michelle.

"What's going on, little one?" he asked, as they entered their house. "You haven't said a word, and you look like you're ready to bite someone."

"I'm fine, Daddy," she snarled, "There's nothing going on."

"And I'm not buying it, Shelly," Pete said. "So either give with a smile or tell me what's wrong."

"You're not buying what?" Marybelle asked as she came in.

"Nothing!" Michelle said.

"Something," Pete said. "Our daughter seems to be a little put off, though she's not saying."

"What's wrong, Michelle?" Marybelle asked. "Did something happen at the mall?"

"Nothing happened at the mall," Michelle said, "that's the problem."

"Okay, what was supposed to happen?" Pete asked.

"I don't want to talk about it!" Michelle said.

"Too bad," Pete said. "Something's obviously bothering you, so let it out. Maybe we can help."

"You can't," Michelle said. "Not unless you can do something about that stupid Corey Palmer." Michelle slumped down on the sofa, crossing her arms.

"Corey?" Marybelle said, sitting down next to Michelle. "What's he done?"

"He hasn't done a thing," Michelle said, "and that's the problem. He hasn't asked me to go to the dance."

Pete and Marybelle couldn't look at each other, knowing they'd both start laughing if they did.

"It's not fair," Michelle continued. "He should have asked ages ago, and could have done it today. But he was too wrapped up in that stupid old ring he found to take a hint."

She stomped off toward her room.

"Oh dear," Marybelle said, beginning to laugh. Pete joined in.

"I think we actually have a teenager," Pete said.

Though the families shared a pew at church the next morning, Corey and Michelle made sure to sit as far apart as possible. They didn't speak either. In the parking lot afterwards, Annette asked Marybelle if she knew what was happening.

"Honey, you will not believe it," Marybelle said. "But here goes. It seems Michelle is mad because Corey hasn't asked her to the dance."

"Are you serious?" Annette asked, laughing.

"I swear to god," Marybelle said. "I haven't seen Shelly so mad since we grounded them over getting stuck in the clock tower. What did Corey tell you?"

"Nothing at all," Annette said. "But it makes sense."

"Can we do anything about it?" Marybelle asked.

Annette thought for a few seconds. "Leave it to me," she said. "I've got an idea."

"You know something, Annette," Marybelle said, as they started moving to their cars. "This is sort of funny, but it's also kind of serious. They're growing up on us, aren't they?"

"Yes, they are," Annette replied.

Chapter IX

On Monday, Brenda Shelton called Rich Geltsin at the *Record / Times*.

"Why not look through your old files?" the editor asked.

"They're not organized," Shelton said. "I'm told the paper always ran the police calls, and I think they'd be easier to look through."

"You might be right about that," Geltsin said. "At least the papers would be chronological. Do you know what timeframe you're looking for?"

"I do. The medical examiner's report stated the body was in the lake for about fifty years, give or take. I figured I'd start around forty years ago and work back."

"Hold on," Geltsin cut in, "is this about the body those kids found in Lake Cyrus?"

"That's right," Shelton replied. "I'm helping the county detectives investigate."

"Alright," Geltsin said, "I'll let you look. But only on two conditions."

"What conditions?" Shelton became wary. The editor was well known for cutting clever deals.

"First, I get copies of your files, including any follow-up from other sources."

"I can't do that."

"Sure you can, officer. It will all become public record eventually anyway."

"So you can wait until then."

"Why should I? You want help from me; you need to give me something."

"Come on," Shelton said, "I'd get in trouble with both the sheriff and my chief if I did."

"Then I'll go over their heads," Geltsin said. "Judge Danielson seems to like me and I'll bet I can get him to order the information released."

"No you can't, it's an on-going investigation."

"Then I'll say no to you and get those kids working on it," Geltsin said. "Now that I know what you're looking for…"

"Alright!" Shelton said. "You win. What's the second condition?"

"I get the exclusive. If there's a story here, I want it."

Shelton agreed and they set an appointment for later that afternoon, after she finished her shift.

***

That morning, Annette told Corey quite firmly to come directly to the courthouse after school.

"Aw, Mom," he said. "Why? Can't I just come home like usual?"

"Aw nothing, Corey," Annette replied. "Just come to the judge's chambers."

The day didn't improve for Corey. Michelle wouldn't speak to him, and neither did Renee or Paula. Tim Crane sat with him during lunch, but wasn't helpful.

"You have to do something, Palmer," Tim said, "or people will start talking. I don't think you want all the girls mad at you."

"Is it that bad?" Corey asked.

"Not yet," Tim said, "but it'll start unless you make it right."

"What should I do?"

"I don't know. You know Michelle better than me, but I've never seen her this angry before. I'm not even sure she'd go with you, even if you do ask."

Corey went straight to the courthouse after school. When he walked into Judge Danielson's office, his mother wasn't there. He asked another person where Annette was, but they didn't know.

Judge Danielson came out of his office.

"Hello, Corey," the judge said. "I'm glad you're here. I talked to your mother today."

"About what?"

"About you and your friend, Michelle."

Corey closed his eyes, counting to ten.

"Let's grab a soda and talk a walk, shall we?" Judge Danielson said.

A few minutes later they were sitting on one of the benches down the hallway.

"Why don't you tell me what happened, Corey," Danielson began.

"Nothing happened," Corey said. "Michelle just got mad at me."

"I heard there's more to it," the judge replied.

"So what?" Corey said. "It's nobody else's business anyway."

"That's not true, Corey. A lot of people care about you, and about Michelle. So they worry if something's not right.

"And things are definitely not right with you two," Danielson continued. "At least from what I've heard."

"It's my problem," Corey said. "What's it to you?"

"Sir," he continued after seeing the judge's stern look.

Danielson shifted to face Corey. "For one thing, your mom asked me to talk to you. She thought you might be more comfortable talking to a man about this.

"And for another, both you and Michelle are my friends," the judge continued.

"Aren't you?"

Corey shrugged his shoulders. "I guess so."

"Alright then. Why don't you tell me what's going on and why your best friend is mad at you?"

Corey told Judge Danielson about finding the ring in Lake Cyrus and how Mr. Pritchard helped clean the grime and muck off and about the incident with Tommy Cooper in the cafeteria. The judge already knew about the body they'd found.

"So after we checked all the yearbooks, I took it to Mr. Jason's Jewelry store. He showed me some initials and then I met the others for lunch. I wanted to tell everyone, but they were talking about dresses, and the school dance coming up, and stuff like that.

"That's when Michelle got mad," Corey finished.

Danielson chuckled. "I think I see the problem. You're right, you didn't do anything, but you should have."

"What should I have done?"

"You should have taken the opportunity to ask Michelle to the dance."

"You are going to ask her, aren't you?" the judge said after a few seconds of silence.

"I don't know if she'd go with me now," Corey said.

"Oh, I bet she will. But even so, there's only one way to find out. Go ask her."

Corey sighed heavily. "I guess I should, but I really don't want to."

"We have to do lots of things we don't want to," Danielson said, "but we do them anyway because they matter to others."

"Why couldn't she just ask me?" Corey said.

"It doesn't work that way, Corey," the judge replied, "at least not with every girl or woman I've ever known."

"What do you mean, sir?"

"Well son, I don't understand the female of our kind very well at all. No man ever really does, though we'll spend most of our lives trying to figure them out. But I have learned one thing over the years. Every girl—every woman—wants to feel special. And they want men to show them they are. It's why we still open doors for them, and send flowers, and lots of other things, big and small."

"Like asking them to go to a dance?"

"Yes, like asking them to go to a dance. You see, Corey, when you ask a girl to go out with you, she gets to feel special. She gets to feel she's important to you, that she matters."

Corey thought about this for a few seconds.

"But how come I don't get that?" he asked. "How come I don't get to feel special to her?"

"You will, son, you will," Danielson said. "You'll get to feel special when she says yes."

"Now let's get on back," he continued, standing up. "I'm sure your mother's waiting."

"One more thing," Danielson said as they walked back to his office and chambers. "What are you going to do next with the ring?"

"I guess I'll go back and look at those yearbooks again," Corey said, "now that I've got a new clue with the initials."

"There's an easier way, you know," the judge said.

"What's that?"

"Check old newspapers. They always print lists of graduating classes. And with your initials, it should be easy."

Corey smiled. "Thanks, Judge, that's a great idea."

Driving home, Corey told Annette about his talk with Judge Danielson, and what he said about why he should ask Michelle to the dance.

"Is that what a girl thinks when a boy asks her to go someplace? He asked.

"That's an important part of it, Corey," Annette replied.

"Is that how you felt with Dad?" Corey said.

Annette smiled, remembering her late husband. David Palmer was the nicest and noblest man she'd ever met. Always respectful and considerate. Even though he'd been killed before Corey really knew him, Annette hoped their son inherited those same characteristics.

"Oh yes, sweetheart," she said, "Oh yes."

"Can we stop at the Pritchards on the way home?" Corey asked. "I think I should talk to Michelle."

"They'll be sitting down to dinner," Annette said. "So let's wait until later."

After dinner and after helping clean up, Corey walked the two blocks to Michelle's house. He tried to rehearse how he'd ask her to the dance along the way, but it just made him anxious. By the time he came to their driveway, Corey was seriously thinking about turning around and going home.

He didn't get the chance. Pete saw him walk up.

"Hi, Corey," he said, "what's up?"

"Hi, Mr. Pritchard," Corey said. "I... umm... I..."

Pete wiped his hands on a rag and walked toward Corey.

"Is something wrong?" he asked.

"No," Corey said. He took a deep breath. "I need to talk to Michelle. Is she here?"

"She's inside, helping with dishes, I think. Go on in."

Corey walked through the garage and opened the connecting door to the house.

"Hello," he called. "Can I come in?"

"Marybelle turned from the sink. "Hi, Corey. Sure—come on in."

Michelle turned around too. "What do you want?"

"Be nice, Michelle," her mother said.

"I wanted to talk to you," Corey said. "Can I?"

Michelle shrugged and crossed her arms. But she didn't turn away.

"I know you're mad at me, Shel," Corey said, "and I'm sorry. I didn't mean to make you angry."

Michelle didn't say anything.

"And I would like to go to the dance with you," Corey continued. "I really wouldn't want to go with anybody else.

"So will you go to the dance with me?"

She turned back to finish putting away dishes.

"I'll think about it," she said.

"Michelle Marie!" Marybelle snapped.

"I'm just messing with him, Mom," Michelle said. She turned around.

"Of course I'll go with you, Corey. I don't want to go with anyone else, either."

Corey grinned. "Cool! It'll be a lot of fun. I'll see if my mom can take us, and we can hang with Tim and Paula, and..."

"Corey, don't worry about that," Marybelle said. "We'll get it figured out."

"Yeah, you're right." He turned to go.

"I guess I better get home. I've still got homework and stuff."

"Me too," Michelle said. "Talk to you at school tomorrow."

Corey almost knocked Pete over as he back through the garage and out to the street.

"Did you two scare that boy off for good?" he asked.

"No, Daddy," Michelle said. "Corey just asked me to go to the dance."

A disturbance on Cedar Drive kept several Craigsville police officers busy past shift change, so Shelton rescheduled her meeting with Rich Geltsin for the next morning. She arrived before the editor, drinking coffee while waiting for the editor to arrive.

"Sorry I'm late," Geltsin said as he walked up and unlocked the door. "The morning meetings lasted longer than usual."

"No problems, I hope," Shelton replied.

"Not really. Just getting used to having everything out at the plant. Now I have to have editorial and production meetings back-to-back each morning."

They walked into the dark offices.

"The good thing, though," the editor continued, "is I get them out of the way quick and can be off doing my own work."

Geltsin turned on lights and walked back to the unoccupied desk area.

"Come on back, Officer," he said. Shelton followed him to a desk where they sat.

"Isn't this still the paper's office?" Shelton asked.

"Officially, yes," Geltsin replied. "But we've moved everything out to the new place. Reporters and the classified desk were the last ones to go last spring."

"What will happen to this building?"

"Eventually we'll sell it. Or not—maybe we'll renovate the upper floors and rent the space out. But we won't do anything until we figure out what to do with the morgue in the basement."

"And that's why I'm here," Shelton said.

"Indeed," Geltsin said, standing up. "So let me show you the layout and help you get started."

"Actually, sir," Shelton said, "I have to report for duty in a few minutes. I'm on days this week."

"I figured there'd be timing issues, but I've got a solution. In the meantime, it will only take a couple of minutes to show you what you need to know."

Geltsin led the officer to the stairway. He flipped on lights as they went down, telling Shelton what each switch controlled. In the large basement space, he told the officer how everything was organized on the shelves, showed her where the issues from the years she wanted would be, and pointed out the work table space.

"The soda machine upstairs still works, and so do the restrooms," the editor said as they went back upstairs. "But feel free to bring your own drinks. Just try not to spill anything down there."

"I won't," Shelton said. "But how often can I come by and look? What times can things be available?"

Geltsin reached into his pocket. "When you cancelled yesterday, I figured this could be a problem. So here's a key to the place, and you can come and go as you need."

"Are you sure?"

"Don't worry. We still use the place now and then to file stories or do research downstairs, so if someone's here, fine. If not, you can have access when you need it."

At the front door, Shelton locked up, proving her key worked, and then shook the editor's hand.

"Thank you for your help," she said.

"Good luck, Officer Shelton," Geltsin said, "but remember our deal."

***

At lunch that day, Paula Terrill never sat down. She ate her sandwich as she went from table to table, rounding up all the dance committee members. They would meet after school that afternoon to start finalizing all the details. Though only an eighth grader, Paula ran the committee when the ninth grader chairing it got sick and missed two weeks of school. Tim was taking her to the dance, but tried to stay out of the way.

"Has she drafted you to help?" Corey asked Tim as they ate their food with Michelle and Renee.

"She's tried, but I can't keep up," Tim answered.

"She's doing a great job," Michelle said. "The dance is going to be special."

"Speaking of which," Renee said to Michelle, "Did someone finally ask you to go?"

"Yes, someone finally did." Michelle winked at Corey.

"Can we ask who?" Renee continued. She looked directly at Corey, who began turning red.

"Who do you think?" Michelle said, coming to Corey's rescue. Tim and Renee laughed.

"Hey, speaking of which, Renee," Tim said, "did anyone ask you?"

"No," Renee answered, "but I'm going. I asked Johnny Draper and he said yes."

"You're kidding!" Michelle said. "I thought he'd be going with Tonya."

"They broke up," Renee said. "So I jumped at the opportunity."

"Hey, Palmer," Tim said. "Are you okay? You're awfully quiet."

"Sorry," Corey said, "just thinking about something else."

"What's up?"

"Just another idea to research that old ring. Judge Danielson suggested we look through old newspapers. He said they always used to print a list of graduates."

"Good idea," Michelle said. "I'm sure Mr. Geltsin will let us."

"Do you want to come with me to the paper?" Corey asked.

"Sure, but you probably want to call first."

Corey called the editor as the bell rang and everyone got up. He left a message, making sure to say his phone would be off until after school let out for the day.

Chapter X

Rich Geltsin left Corey a message to call whenever he could. Corey did as he and Michelle walked from the building to catch their ride for the day.

"Hello, Woodward," Geltsin said, "is Bernstein with you?"

"Huh?" Corey replied.

"Never mind," Geltsin said, chuckling. "An old newspaper joke from before your time. Heck, pretty much before my time. Anyway, what can I do for you, Corey?"

"Well sir, Michelle and I wanted to see if we could look through some more old newspapers."

"What have you got?" the editor asked. "Is this connected to the body you found in the lake?"

"No, sir," Corey said. "We're not working on that. The sheriff sort of told us not to."

Geltsin chuckled.

"We found an old class ring out at the lake, too," Corey continued, "and want to find out who it belonged to."

"And how will old copies of the *Record / Times* help?"

"Didn't the paper always print list of the graduating classes?"

"As a matter of fact..." Geltsin paused.

"Come on down," he continued. "I can meet you there in thirty minutes."

The kids asked Renee's dad to drop them at the courthouse. They would check in with Annette and then go over to the paper's office.

Geltsin arrived just before the kids. He welcomed them and took them back to a desk.

"Alright, what have you got this time?"

Corey took the pictures from his backpack. "I found this ring the same day we found that body. It's from the US Naval Academy and there are initials inside."

"The year on the ring is nineteen sixty-five," Michelle said, "so we figure whoever it belongs to graduated from high school in nineteen sixty-one."

"Mr. Jason at the jewelry store looked at it and he made out the initials of *PMS* on the inside," Corey added.

"We looked through old yearbooks," Michelle said, "but couldn't find anyone who went to the Naval Academy."

"Judge Danielson told me the paper always printed lists of graduating classes," Corey said.

"So we want to look at those papers," Michelle said.

Geltsin put up his hands. "Enough! Do you two practice this routine? You're harder to follow than a good tennis match."

"And yes, you can look through the papers," he continued. "It should be easy. We print the lists the week after each high school graduates, so all you'll have to check is the first or second week of June."

"Will all the high schools be there?" Michelle asked.

"All the ones for Wagner and Jameson counties," Geltsin said. "You'll have to look up the *Morris Mercury* for Morris County and maybe Cherokee, too."

"Do you have copies of those issues?" Corey asked.

"Nope," Geltsin said. "But they went digital a few years ago. All their back issues are on the web. You can look them up yourself."

"When can we start looking?" Michelle asked.

"Right now if you want," Geltsin said. "It's not going to take you long, and you know how things work down there. Go on down and look."

Corey and Michelle got up.

"But there are a couple of other things you should think about," the editor said. "First off, you might want to check a couple of other years."

"Why?" Corey asked.

"Do you know how someone gets into the Naval Academy, or any of the other military schools?"

"No," Michelle said, "not really."

"You have to get an appointment," Geltsin explained. "Or get in under some special situations. Most people get an appointment from a member of Congress and go in right after high school.

"But sometimes not. Sometimes a person couldn't get an appointment after graduating, but they would reapply the next year. Or they'd go to a prep school so they could pass the entrance exams and then get an appointment. So it's possible your person could have graduated in nineteen sixty or fifty-nine."

"Should we look farther back?" Corey asked.

"Probably not," Geltsin said.

"What's the other thing?" Michelle asked.

"Why not just check the Naval Academy records?" Geltsin replied. "Go at it from the other side."

"I didn't know we could do that," Corey said.

"Sure you can. It's public record," Geltsin said. "They might not have old records online, but it would certainly be worth checking. It would save you a lot of time."

"I'd still check the papers, though," the editor continued, "that way you'd have a solid connection and a trail."

The kids headed downstairs to the paper's morgue.

They quickly found the boxes with June issues for the three years in question. At the work table, each took one year and began looking for the issues with list of graduating classes. The work went fast as the front page noted if a list was printed inside.

The print was small, but knowing the initials made it easy. Corey found several names from nineteen sixty-one and wrote them down. Michelle didn't find any name to match the letters from nineteen fifty-nine, but wasn't surprised. She grabbed the next year to finish.

As she did, Officer Shelton came down the stairs. Both kids looked up.

"Hi kids," Shelton said, "Mr. Geltsin said you were down here."

"Hi, Officer," Michelle said. "What's up?"

"I suspect the same thing that's up with you," Shelton replied. "Research. I need to look through old papers."

"What are you looking for?" Corey asked.

"Well, I'd usually say I can't comment, but since you two are responsible, I don't see any harm. I'm looking for any report of someone missing from about forty-five years ago."

"You're looking into the body we found, aren't you?" Michelle asked.

"Yes I am," Shelton said, "I'm helping the county detectives."

"Can we help?" Corey asked.

"Corey!" Michelle said.

"Actually, I'd love some help," Shelton said. "I'm going to start with forty years ago and work backward. So it's going to be a lot of work."

"What do we need to do?" Corey asked.

"Let me show you," Shelton said. She retrieved a box from a shelf and came back to the table. Opening it, she spread out the old papers.

"The paper prints what's called the police blotter. It's a summary of all the sheriff and city police calls since the last time. I'm looking for anything about someone being reported missing."

She opened an issue. "The good news is the paper's index lists where to look right on the first page. But the bad news is every issue has to be checked."

"How far back?" Michelle asked.

"Probably ten years," Shelton said. "At least that's what the medical examiner's initial report said."

"Wow," Corey said.

"So do you still want to help?" Shelton asked.

"I do," Corey said. "It might be fun, reading about what happened back then."

"What about you, Michelle?"

Michelle thought for a few seconds. "I don't know. I don't think Sheriff Wingate wants us to get involved in this."

"Don't worry, he won't find out from me," Shelton said. "And anyway, you two found the body, so it ought to be your case.

"Okay," Michelle said. "But not every day."

"I can't do it every day either," Shelton said, "In fact, I just wanted to get a start today. Sort of get organized. I've got tomorrow and Saturday off, but regular shifts on the other days this week."

"How can we get together?" Corey asked.

"I'll give you my phone number," Shelton said, "or you can just call the police station. I'll let you know if I'm available and going to work down here."

"Cool," Corey said, "but I can't help tomorrow. I have to go to the mall with my mom."

"What for?"

"I'm getting a new suit for the dance," Corey said. "And it had to be altered. We're going to see if it fits right."

"Ah yes, the dance," Shelton said. "Are you going, Michelle?"

"Uh-huh. And I got a new dress, too."

"Maybe we could help during the day on Saturday, before the dance," Corey said.

"Maybe you can, Corey," Michelle said. "But I've already got plans. My dad is pulling the engine from his old Ford Torino and I get to help. I'd rather do that."

"So would I," Shelton said. "Wouldn't you, Corey?"

"I don't know," Corey said. "I mean it's a great old car and everything, but this would be helping to solve a mystery."

"Oh come on, Corey," Shelton said. "These old papers will still be here, but how often do you get the chance to go elbows deep into a two-eighty-nine V-8 engine?"

"Three-oh-two," the kids said together.

"See?" Shelton said, laughing. "Anyway, you two can start helping next week after school. And if I find something before then, I'll let you know Saturday night at the dance."

"You're going to our dance?" Michelle asked.

"Yes. Mr. Isaacs asked me to go."

"You mean you're going as his…?" Corey said.

"I'm going as another chaperone," Shelton interrupted.

"Well yeah, but…" Corey continued.

"But nothing, young man," Shelton said. "Mr. Isaacs happens to be my brother. I'm just doing him a favor.

"And I'm still a police officer, so you'd better behave."

Michelle finished looking through the June, nineteen sixty back issues, finding a couple of possibilities. She wrote these down while Corey began looking through a few issues with Officer Shelton. They left after that.

Shelton made it through nineteen seventy-four on her days off, though she didn't find any report matching the dead man's characteristics. She'd pick up her search with the previous year the next week.

**

Later in the week, Annette and Marybelle finalized arrangements. Annette would drive the kids to the dance, with Corey picking up Michelle. Some traditions still mattered, the women decided. The Pritchards would pick them up afterwards.

"You won't recognize him," Annette told her friend. "He looks like a young lawyer. The dark gray suit, white shirt and striped tie make him look grown up and handsome."

She'd insisted on buying a size too large, so the tailor could leave a lot of material in the seams and hems. If Corey would just stop growing so fast, she told Marybelle, he might get a couple of years out of the thing.

"Wait 'til he sees Michelle," Marybelle said.

She was perfectly sized for the dress they'd chosen, even though it probably wouldn't see another year.

"I swear, Annette," Marybelle said, sighing, "They're growing up too fast. Only thirteen and going on a real date."

Annette laughed. "It's just a school dance. And besides, at least they're going together."

The rest of the week passed quietly for Corey and Michelle. They helped pull things together for Saturday's dance and Paula didn't drive anyone too crazy with instructions. By the end of school Friday, the cafeteria was decorated in streamers and autumn décor. A stage was set up at one end and chairs set along the walls. A few tables were set around also, for the small refreshments. Final preparations would happen Saturday morning.

***

Dr. Driscoll's week was very productive. She got some results back from colleagues and another report from the state lab. Stuart Byrd sent a more complete write-up with no new developments but lots of details and conclusions on the boat and some information on the soil.

Gerry Peterson called from Cherokee County.

"Just wanted to thank you for this," he said. "My new GCMS got a good workout."

"Did you find anything interesting?" Driscoll asked.

"On the paint and such, no," Peterson replied. "I determined the year, nineteen sixty-one, for the paint and the metal. The lead content told me that, and I think that tag Birdie found is an ID of some kind. Could be a manufacturer's."

"What about the soil samples?"

"Nothing out of the ordinary. Some residue of fertilizer runoff, but that's probably old. Mostly minerals and elements we see all around us. I'll know more when I run them again."

"What about the tissue samples? Any luck there?"

"Not if you're looking for an ID," Peterson said. "I was able to create a complete DNA profile, but without anything to compare to, you're out of luck."

"That's okay," Driscoll said. "I didn't expect anything. But a complete profile is more than I can do. And it will be a point of reference. Anything else?"

"Nope. Your victim was a healthy Caucasian male, probably in his twenties or thirties. But you knew that, didn't you, Mo?"

"Yes I did."

"And, he might have drowned. He could have been alive when he went into the lake. But I suspect you knew that, too."

"I did, Gerry, but thanks just the same. Everything helps. Can you send me a written version?"

"I will, but I've still got some other tests. I might as well see what my new friend can really do."

Driscoll didn't like not making more progress. Though her colleagues were providing much needed detail, she still didn't know anything about the dead man. She needed some place to start.

By Friday, she'd gathered everything together and created a new and larger case file. Before leaving for the weekend, she dropped copies off to the sheriff's office and the city police, and emailed a summary to Rich Geltsin.

***

Saturday didn't start well for Corey. He didn't make it to Michelle's until almost noon as Annette had him doing chores all morning. Including cutting the grass, for what he hoped was the last time this season. Unfortunately, there would soon be leaves to rake.

As he walked up to the Pritchard's garage, Corey saw Mr. Pritchard working to adjust the tripod rig holding the engine. When ready, he'd be able to pull the motor all the way out of the car's body. Michelle's thin legs protruded from under the car.

Pete looked up as Corey approached. "Hi, Corey, glad you could make it."

"Ouch," Michelle said from under the car.

"You okay, Shel?" Pete asked.

"Yes, but I can't hold this and remove the bolts. I need help."

"What are you trying to do?" Corey asked as he knelt down.

"Trying to get the oil pan off," Michelle answered. "It's in the way."

"That's something you can do, Corey," Pete said. "Crawl under and hold the pan while Michelle unbolts it."

Corey did as the next few hours passed quickly. Once the engine was disconnected and hoisted high enough to work without climbing into it, they began disassembling in piece by piece.

"Okay, kids," Pete said after a while. "Now comes a tricky part. I'm going to remove the camshaft and the driveshaft, and I'll need you to pull the rocker arms out as I disconnect them.

"Then I'll need you to grab onto the piston heads and hold them so they don't fall back through."

"Should we pull the pistons out?" Michelle asked.

"Yes, but carefully," Pete answered. "If they won't slide easily, leave them. We'll deal with them later."

The job went smoothly, though two pistons were stuck fast. At four thirty, Corey had to leave. He needed to go home, eat some dinner, clean up and then come back with Annette to pick Michelle up for the dance.

Annette inspected her son as they left the house.

"You are quite the handsome young man," she said. "You look grown up and ready for the world. I suspect Judge Danielson would think he's in for an interesting argument if you showed up in his court."

"Aw, Mom," Corey said, "he's knows me too well."

"Judge Barker, then," Annette said, chuckling. She then made sure Corey remembered the wrist corsage they'd bought for Michelle.

Marybelle greeted them at the Pritchard's front door. "You look very distinguished, Mr. Palmer," she said. Corey blushed.

Annette and Corey stood in the living room as Marybelle went to get Michelle. As she entered the room, Annette gasped and Corey's eyes grew wide.

Michelle was dressed in a straight black dress with thin shoulder straps. Her hair was pulled back into a tight knot high on the back of her head with long curling strands framing her face. The dress ended mid-thigh, showing off her thin and tanned legs. She wore black shoes with short heels and long gloves on each arm.

"Wow..." Corey said. "Wow... You look... Umm... You're... Uh... Oh man..."

"I think Corey's trying to say you look very nice," Annette said.

"More than that," Corey said, "You look..." He couldn't find the words.

"She looks beautiful?" Marybelle offered.

"Gorgeous?" Pete added.

"I don't have a word," Corey said. "What comes next?"

"Stop it," Michelle said. "You're all embarrassing me."

Corey remembered the corsage. "I got this for you, but I don't know if it will work with the gloves."

"You can blame me for those," Pete said. "A bit of a mishap after you left."

"What happened?" Corey asked.

"We were cleaning the camshaft and some solvent splashed on my hand," Michelle said. "It's just a chemical burn."

"But gauze wouldn't look good with that dress," Pete said.

They decided the corsage looked fine, even with the gloves. After taking a few pictures, Annette and the kids left for the school.

"See you around eleven," Pete said as they departed.

Chapter XI

Cars lined the drive at the school's entrance as parents dropped off their well-dressed kids in various combinations. Most left soon after, but some of the adults began talking, and soon newer arrivals began honking to get them moving. One group of parents was heading to the movies and some others were going back to a potluck dinner. Annette was joining that group, after stopping back home to pick up some cookies she'd baked.

"Have fun, you two," she told Corey and Michelle. "Call if you need anything."

"We will, Mom," Corey said. They headed inside.

Officially, the dance began at eight o'clock. That's when Mr. Dorsey took the stage and welcomed everyone. He kept it short, turning the microphone over to Paula for the real start.

"Hi, everyone," Paula said to the crowd. "It's great to see you all and I hope everybody has a great time tonight. I just wanted to thank all the kids who helped organize and set things up. We worked really hard, and hope you think it was worth it."

Paula paused for a second as a few kids clapped.

"Okay, now it's time to get things going, so here's our DJ for the night, Charlie Clyde."

Charlie played a few bars of music, then added his own welcome.

"Hello, kids, it's great to be here tonight. I've got lots of music for you, and I do take requests. Come on up and look through my lists and write down what you'd like to hear. I've got old stuff, new stuff, and even some non-country."

Some older kids laughed.

"So let's get the dancing started, shall we?" He cued up the first song.

Tim, Renee, and Johnny Draper waited with Corey and Michelle for Paula to rejoin them. None of them wanted to dance to this first number.

"Why on earth did you get that old geezer as the DJ?" Johnny asked Paula when she arrived.

"He works cheap," Paula said. "Free, actually. We were supposed to have one of the other station guys, but they dropped out at the last minute. So Mr. Clyde is filling in."

"Well I hope he plays some stuff we can dance to," Tim said.

"Let's hope," Paula said.

Throughout the first half-hour, everyone talked, munched on the refreshments, and generally behaved. There were no fights or loud words, at least none loud enough to bring the chaperones.

Principal Dorsey didn't stay around. He liked to trust his students to conduct themselves well without watching over their shoulders. There were about ten adults present anyway, a mix of parents, teachers with their spouses, and one police officer. Mr. Dorsey knew Officer Shelton was there with her brother, Mr. Isaacs. Uniformed security personnel were outside, but wouldn't come in unless called.

Most of the kids stayed in small groups of just boys or just girls. Some, like Corey and Michelle, or Tim and Paula, paired as couples, but still stayed at tables or along the walls.

The adults stayed to themselves, talking to students when they came near, but hung out along the walls for the most part. Hardly anyone danced to anything Charlie played until a secret request from an adult couple finally kick-started things.

"Well now, here's a very special request that's probably older than all of us put together," he said. "I have no idea what's up, but hope you enjoy." He cued up *American Patrol* by Glenn Miller's orchestra.

Two adult couples trotted to the center of the dance floor and began showing off some ballroom dance steps straight out of the nineteen thirties. They spun, dipped, and threw some high kicking flourishes. For a few seconds, most of the kids just gaped, but then a group of ninth grade girls began clapping to the beat. Soon, everyone was clapping along and bobbing their heads. At the end, the couples took a bow to loud applause. That broke the ice. Charlie played some fast numbers and the kids started to dance.

Even twelve and thirteen year-olds need a break now and then, so Charlie played a slow number after a while. Corey and Michelle were on the floor when the soft love song began. Michelle moved close to him.

"I don't really know how to do this," he said.

"It's okay. We can do what my dad calls the hanging shuffle." She put her arms around his neck and he put his around her waist. They didn't pull close, but swayed to the music, moving their feet occasionally.

Corey tried hard not to kick Michelle's feet, but wasn't completely successful.

As the second verse began, Mike Bates come over and shoved Corey away.

"I'm cutting in," he said. "I'll show you how it's really done." He grabbed Michelle around the waist and pulled her close. Before Corey could do anything, they'd moved away.

Not wanting to be left alone or make a scene, Corey began moving back to the tables off the dance floor.

Michelle danced stiffly with the older boy. He wasn't bad, and did seem to know some steps. After a few seconds though, Michelle felt his hand move below her waist, down toward the top of her thigh.

"Stop it," she said, grabbing his wrist to move the hand back up.

A few seconds later, she felt the hand down here again. This time, Mike squeezed her bottom. Michelle pushed him off.

"I said stop it!" she said loudly. "Stop trying to feel me up!"

"Aw, come on, girl," Mike said with a leer. "You know you like it. You're asking for it, with that get-up."

"I am not!" Michelle said, as she started walking away.

Mike grabbed her arm. "You don't just walk away from me, slut. Come here." He tried to pull her back.

The noise made other couples around them stop and watch. Over at the tables, Corey moved toward them as he saw Mike grab Michelle.

"Leave me alone!" Michelle cried, wrenching her arm free.

Mike raised his right hand to strike Michelle. Corey saw this.

"Hey!" he called out. It distracted Mike for a moment and Michelle used the opportunity to aim a hard and fast kick.

Her foot made full contact with the most vulnerable and sensitive part of Mike's anatomy. The young man expelled all his breath, doubled over in agony and collapsed to the floor just as Corey arrived.

"Are you okay?" he asked Michelle.

"I'm good," she said, "I got this."

"Yeah," Corey said. "Wow."

Others reacted to the uproar, too. Officer Shelton and Mr. Isaacs came over, arriving just after Corey.

"What's going on here?" Isaacs asked.

"He couldn't keep his hands to himself," Michelle answered. "I dealt with him."

"She sure did," Corey said, smiling.

Officer Shelton knelt next to Mike. "You'll be alright, young man, just take deep breaths." She smiled up at Michelle and winked.

Mike's breathing slowed and his body relaxed. In a minute, he could stand again. Tommy Cooper and Joey Halston came over and helped their friend walk back to a table. No one spoke, but Tommy gave Michelle a fierce look.

"You want something, Cooper?" Michelle said, angrily. "I can give you some of the same."

"That's enough!" Mr. Isaacs said. "It's over. Let's everyone go back to dancing."

"Why don't we step outside?" Officer Shelton said, "And let things settle down."

Corey, Michelle, and the two adults made their way out of the building to the courtyard. Michelle was still angry.

"I don't believe that jackass!" she said. "He was trying to feel me up, running his hands over my thigh and even squeezing my ass.

"I mean, what makes him think he can do that? Did he just think I'd let him?"

"I hope not," Shelton said.

"What then?" Michelle went on. "Would he try to reach up under my dress next?"

Isaacs and Corey both blushed. This wasn't Michelle's usual language.

"What was I supposed to do about it?"

"You were pretty effective back there," Shelton said. "I doubt anyone else tries it."

"Yeah, but am I going to have to kick my way out of every situation?" Michelle said.

Shelton thought for a few seconds. "I don't know what was going through that boy's mind, Michelle, but unfortunately, most boys his age think that way. It's the nature of their hormones."

"It doesn't make it right," Michelle said.

"That's true," Shelton replied. "And there is no excuse for what he did. It was wrong and he needs to learn a lesson.

"The thing is, it will take time. At least it does for most boys. Eventually, most of them grow up and their brains begin to function."

"But what do I do in the meantime?" Michelle asked. "They're bigger than me, and they act like they're entitled. They're all jerks."

"I'm not that way," Corey said.

"That's because you know better," Michelle said sharply. "You know what I can do to you."

"Take it easy, Michelle," Shelton said. "I think Corey's on your side here."

"Listen, respecting others is something we all have to learn. It isn't something we're born with. Unfortunately, some people—boys particularly—don't learn it until later."

"If they ever do," she continued. "It's going to be hard for you, but you can do something about it."

"Like what?"

"Like what you did back there. Stand up. Stand your ground, and make it clear you won't tolerate it."

"But what if they turn mean, like Bates did," Michelle said, "or like Tommy Cooper's always trying with me?"

"Ask for help," Mr. Isaacs said. "Most people will be on your side, even if you don't think so."

"I'm on your side, Shel," Corey said. "I'll help."

Michelle let her shoulders sag. She looked at the adults and then at her best friend.

"Okay," she said. "And at least stupid ol' Mikey Bates will keep his hands off me."

"Speaking of which," Shelton asked, "where did you learn that trick?"

"My mom taught me."

The adults laughed.

A siren pierced the air. They all knew the sound of the fire alarm.

"What the…"

Isaacs and Shelton reacted quickly. "Stay here, you two," the officer said as the adults starting running toward the door.

Inside, the alarm was louder. On stage, Charlie Clyde's fingers flew over his laptop and console. He always prepared for this, though he'd never needed the music he now cued up. The fast opening of *Stars & Stripes Forever* blasted from the speakers.

"Alright, everyone," Charlie said calmly over the blaring march. "You can hear the siren and the music. Let's get moving. Stay calm and orderly, but everyone needs to get outside now. Let's go, go, move it, now."

The kids began exiting the building in pretty good order. No one screamed, though several wondered if it was real. It might be a false alarm, someone said.

In his office, the school principal heard the alarm and looked up. Without thinking, he called 9-1-1 and reported it. After hanging up, Mr. Dorsey began wondering if there really was a fire, or just a false alarm. Some prankster might have left the cafeteria and pulled an alarm just for kicks.

But with over two-thirds of his students at the dance, he thought, he couldn't take the chance.

Dorsey left his office and headed for the cafeteria. He first needed to make sure everyone was out and safe.

Shelton and Isaacs had to fight through the crowd to get back into the building. They made it the stage just as Charlie shut the music off and began pulling cables, gathering CDs, and shutting down his laptop and console.

"What's happening?" Isaacs asked.

"No clue," Charlie said. "I heard the alarm and told the kids to leave."

"Do you know where the alarm is coming from?" Shelton asked.

"It sounds like somewhere farther in the building. But I couldn't say. Sorry, but I need to save my music."

"Thanks for your help," Shelton said, "I think everyone's out."

Charlie grabbed his console, laptop, and CD carriers. He'd worry about the speakers later. They were easier to replace.

"Let's go," Isaacs said, "we need to find where the fire is, if there is one." They left the cafeteria and moved into the hallway.

Outside, Tim and Paula found Corey and Michelle. No one knew what was really happening. Corey was standing on the outdoor table, looking around. He saw smoke coming from beyond the corner of the building.

"Look over there, guys," he said. "It's coming from around the corner."

The others looked to where he pointed.

"Something's burning," Tim said.

"Let's go see," Corey said, climbing down.

"It might not be safe," Michelle said.

"But we might be able to help," Corey said, moving away. "Come on."

As they rounded the corner, they could see smoke coming from an open window toward the other end of the building. Two boys were getting up from the ground.

"That's the science room," Paula said.

"Hey!" Corey called to the now running boys. "*Hey!*"

Neither turned and both kept running toward the back part of the school property.

"Do you think they started it?" Tim asked.

"Probably," Corey said. "But we'll never catch them."

"We need to tell someone," Michelle said. They could hear the different sirens of the fire trucks arriving.

"I'll go back," Paula said. "You guys try to see how bad it is."

Inside, Mr. Dorsey, Mr. Isaacs, Officer Shelton, and two other teachers all made it to the science room hallway. The door was closed, but they saw smoke coming from underneath it.

"Not good," Dorsey said. "That's the most dangerous room in the school. We need to tell the fire department and then get everyone farther away."

"But the room has its own sprinkler system," one of the teachers said. "Why didn't they put the fire out?"

"That's a question for later," Lieutenant Franks of the Craigsville Fire Dept. said as he and two firefighters came down the hall. "Right now, we need to get it under control." Franks and one of the others carried axes, while the third carried a large fire extinguisher.

"You folks need to go outside and let us handle this."

"How did you know where the fire was?" Dorsey asked.

"A girl outside told us."

Corey, Michelle and Tim approached the window bent low. The smoke wasn't heavy, but was consistent. It rose quickly in the outside air. Being the tallest, Corey could look over the edge standing flat. He looked into the room.

"What do you see?" Michelle asked.

"There's lots of smoke, but I don't see a lot of flame. The sprinklers are running, so everything is getting soaked."

"So what's still burning?" Tim asked as he joined Corey.

"I don't know," Corey said. "Hold it—there are some jets of flame coming from something on one of the lab tables."

"It's the gas for the Bunsen burners," Michelle said. Corey and Tim stood away.

"We've got to shut it off," she continued.

"How can we do that?" Tim asked.

"The gas lines," Corey said. "Come on." He took off toward the next corner of the building.

Michelle slipped off her shoes to run. She caught up with Corey as he got to the corner.

As they turned the corner, a fire engine arrived outside the science room. The firefighters told Tim to move aside.

"It's burning gas," he told them.

A firefighter looked in the window, then he keyed his radio.

"Command, this is engine two. We got gas jets burning. The suppression system is going, but not putting the fire out. We need to cut the gas."

"Copy, two," Franks replied. He turned to Mr. Dorsey. "What kind of gas jets are in there, and where's the cutoff?"

"The gas is for Bunsen burners," Dorsey replied. "It shouldn't explode, but the cutoff for this room is under the teacher's table. Can't you go in and turn it off?"

"No sir," the lieutenant answered. "If we open this door, the cross-venting might make the fire grow. You've heard of a back draft, haven't you? This is similar."

Franks keyed his radio. "Two, this is command. We need entry and then access to a cutoff valve under the front table. Can your crew get in through the window?"

"Yes, sir. We're on it." Two crew members helped their colleague check his full breathing apparatus.

Corey and Michelle came to the series of tanks and pipes fuelling the building. The school used natural gas for its heat, and the main line entered the building here. There were large and small tanks holding other fuels. One was the gas used in the science room.

"Which one do we turn off?" Michelle asked.

"I don't know," Corey answered, "Let's just turn off all the valves."

The valves were easy to turn, and they had every one closed within a minute.

The firefighter in full gear began climbing through the window. Looking for a place to put his leading foot, he saw the streams of burning gas die out.

"Command, this is two," he radioed. "Either the source burned out or someone beat us to it. The gas is off. We'll bring a hose in and cool everything down."

"Copy that," Franks answered. He turned to Dorsey.

"Is there anything in there we should be worried about?"

"I can get you a current inventory, but everything should be labeled," the principal said.

"How did you know about this?" Michelle asked Corey as they walked back around the building.

"One of the janitors told me about it."

They came around the corner and rejoined Tim outside the science room. A firefighter noticed them.

"What are you doing here?" he asked.

"We turned off the gas," Corey said.

The man radioed this to Lieutenant Franks.

"Hold onto them," Franks radioed back. "We'll need to hear the whole story."

After hearing this, Corey, Michelle, and Tim began walking back to the courtyard where everyone else was.

"We're in trouble again, aren't we?" Michelle said.

Parents were arriving in droves to pick up the kids. Everyone started calling for rides as soon as they got outside. The dance was well and truly over. Mr. Dorsey told everyone in the courtyard there would be a special assembly first thing Monday morning. A lot needed to be investigated and considered.

"We'll talk about this then," he said. "Please try to enjoy what's left of your weekend."

Corey, Michelle, Tim, and Paula sat on a table, resting their feet on the bench. As their excitement and energy dissipated in the cool evening air, the girls wrapped their arms around themselves. Corey noticed Michelle shiver and removed his jacket, placing it around her shoulders.

"Thanks," she said. Tim took the hint and gave Paula his jacket.

The firefighters quickly had the fire doused and things under control. While a few chemicals might have exploded, none were close to the fire's starting point. Teachers present stayed and helped remove things from the burned room.

Chief Blaise and Sheriff Wingate arrived. Franks gave them an initial report.

"The room where it started is a total loss," he said, "but nothing else was damaged."

"What caused it?" Blaise asked.

"Not sure how it started, but gas fuelled it until turned off. We'll start an arson investigation right away."

"Any witnesses?" Wingate asked.

"A group of kids were outside," Franks said, "but I don't know if they're involved. One of them said they cut off the gas." He directed the officers to the table where the kids still sat. Officer Shelton was with them along with Pete Pritchard, who'd arrived after most all the students were gone.

Wingate and Blaise walked over. Seeing who it was, Wingate stopped.

"I should have known you two were involved."

"We didn't do anything wrong," Corey said. "We even tried to help."

"Hang on, Sheriff," Shelton said. "I know for certain Corey and Michelle weren't part of this. They were with me when the alarm went off, and had been for some time."

"What about these other two?" Blaise asked.

"We were inside, dancing," Paula said. "We joined Corey and Michelle after we came outside."

"Alright," Wingate said, "what's this about turning off the gas?"

"We saw smoke coming from the side of the building," Corey explained, "and when we went to look, we saw it coming from the science room."

"We checked it out and saw the gas jets," Michelle said.

"That's when I came back here to let the fire department know," Paula added.

"And Corey and Michelle ran around the building to shut off the gas," Tim said.

"And I saw a couple of guys climbing out of the room," Corey said.

"Hold it," Officer Shelton said. "I didn't know that. Did you recognize them?"

"No, ma'am," Corey said. "I didn't see their faces. But I'm pretty sure they weren't any of the kids at the dance."

"How can you know that?" Chief Blaise asked.

"They were dressed in jeans and hoodies," Corey answered. "No one at the dance was dressed that way."

"That's good, Corey," Shelton said, as the other officers made notes. "It will help."

"How'd you know which valve to shut off?" Wingate asked.

"We didn't," Michelle said. "We shut them all off."

"That's good, kids," Chief Blaise said. "Good job. There will probably be more questions later, but go on home for now." He and Sheriff Wingate walked away.

"I've got a question now," Tim said. "Why did the DJ play that crazy music when the fire alarm went off?"

"That's a little history lesson for you," Mr. Isaacs said as he rejoined the group. He'd helped clean up the science room and dance.

"You see, back in the days of travelling circuses and a canvas big top, Sousa's march was the ultimate distress call. When the band played *Stars & Stripes Forever*, it meant everyone in the company needed to come running. There's a major disaster. It also meant get the people out, fast.

"I suppose Charlie Clyde knew the story, and had the march ready just in case he needed to get people moving. Folks pay attention to it."

"Is it still used that way today?" Michelle asked.

"In the circus, yes," Isaacs replied. "But I don't think so anywhere else. Fire alarms are pretty loud."

After dropping Tim and Paula off, Pete drove the kids back to the Pritchards. With the evening's excitement, Annette came over to hear the details. Around the kitchen table, Corey and Michelle began telling what happened and how they ended up playing a part in the fire and its aftermath.

"You really kicked that boy in the…" Marybelle said.

"She really did," Corey said. "You should have seen it. Old Mikey collapsed in a heap."

"He deserved it, Mom," Michelle said. "He was trying to feel me up."

"Where were you, Corey?" Annette asked.

"I was coming over to help. But Shel didn't need any," Corey said. "She took care of it really well."

The women just looked at Michelle, saying nothing.

But Pete Pritchard smiled and said, "That's my girl."

Rich Geltsin called each house on Sunday, wanting details on the fire. They met at the Pritchards, and filled the editor in everything, including Corey's seeing the older boys run from the scene.

"By the way, how's the other research going?" Geltsin asked the kids after finishing with the fire story.

"Slow," Michelle told him.

"We found a few possibilities," Corey said, "but haven't had a chance to work on them."

"You're also helping Officer Shelton, aren't you?" Geltsin asked. "Anything going on there?"

"Not that we've heard," Michelle said. "But we won't start helping her until next week."

Chapter XII

If the fire at Craigsville Middle School wasn't the main topic of conversation through Sunday, Charlie Clyde put it there first thing Monday.

"Good morning, everyone. Welcome back from the weekend and happy Monday. Charlie Clyde with you here on WMCJ, and it looks like this is going to be a permanent thing.

"What a weekend, folks. I'm pretty sure you've all heard about the little flare up we had over in Craigsville on Saturday. But if you haven't, there was a small fire in the middle school's science lab. I happened to be there, playing music for the fall dance, and I'm happy to tell you no one was injured. The kids did a good job getting out of the building too.

"And then on Sunday, we got some big news here at the station. Seems the raging lunatics have finally surfaced. Our old buddies, Louie and Rick are taking their show to a higher level. Mile high, to be exact—the boys now host a morning show in Denver.

"They got married, too. How about that? Now here's Taylor Swift to kick things off."

The *Record / Times* also led with Saturday's fire, providing a few more details. Rich Geltsin called Mr. Dorsey on Sunday for comment, but the principal wouldn't say anything beyond confirming what the editor learned from the sheriff's office and from Corey and Michelle.

At Craigsville Middle School, Principal Dorsey began the day as he promised, holding a school-wide assembly in the auditorium. He didn't spend much time reviewing what happened as most of the kids were there.

"So again, everyone, thank you for evacuating the dance quickly and safely. For those who were not there, it was quite an event."

"Will there be another one?' a seventh grader called out. Some students laughed.

"To be determined," Dorsey replied, smiling.

"Actually, we are still investigating," he continued, more seriously, "and we will be speaking with certain students throughout the day. Most of you already know who you are, so please report to the office when called. Your teachers also know, so there should be no issues. As to the science classes, with the room completely unusable, all classes scheduled there will meet in the cafeteria.

"One last thing. While most of you know what happened after the fire started and the authorities arrived, I don't think anyone knows exactly how things started. So please, let the investigation proceed and don't spread rumors. Thank you."

Dorsey dismissed the kids to a shortened first period.

Michelle didn't make it that far. She was the first student called to the office.

Corey was the last, called out of his English class, to Mrs. Hollis's considerable annoyance.

"Please sit down, Mr. Palmer," Mr. Dorsey said when Corey entered the principal's office. Officer Shelton was also present, along with Detective Ruter.

"I believe you know Officer Shelton well, and this is Detective Ruter with the sheriff's office."

"What would you like to know?" Corey asked nervously.

"We need to know everything you saw," Ruter said. "All the details."

"We really just need to know if you can add anything to what we've heard," Shelton said. "You're our last interview. We've got a pretty good picture of everything."

"Okay," Corey said. He took a breath and told what happened from when Mike Bates cut in on him to how he and Michelle cut off the gas. Detective Ruter raised his eyebrows when Corey mentioned the two boys he saw running away.

"Did you recognize them?" the detective asked.

"No, sir. They didn't turn when I hollered, so I didn't see their faces. I only saw them from the back, but they were wearing jeans and one wore a hoodie."

"Are you sure they weren't students here?"

"Pretty sure," Corey said. "I think they were taller than me and no one at the dance was dressed like that."

Corey couldn't add more, so Mr. Dorsey ended the interview.

"One more thing, Mr. Palmer," he said as Corey rose to leave. "Well done on turning off the gas. Tell Ms. Pritchard the same, too."

Outside, Shelton called Corey to wait a second.

"Can you and Michelle work in the morgue this week?"

"I think so," Corey answered. "I'll have to ask Michelle and we'll need to arrange rides after school."

"Good," the officer replied. "Let's start tomorrow afternoon. I can give you a ride to the square if needed."

"And by the way, Corey," Shelton continued, "tell Michelle 'well done' on that other incident too."

"I will," Corey said, smiling.

Michelle agreed to join Corey and Shelton in the paper's basement after school the next day. They wouldn't need a ride from the officer as Renee's mom would take them down to the square instead of home.

***

In the county morgue, Dr. Driscoll was having a very productive Monday. Several files and follow-up reports arrived that morning, and she spent much of her time reading and learning about the body found in Lake Cyrus.

After reading all the files, she called several of her colleagues. She called the state crime lab first, thanking them for their efforts. Their report didn't tell her anything new, though it did provide great details. These might come in handy later, she thought. Driscoll then called Dr. Byrd in Morris.

"Hi, Birdie," she said, "I just finished your new soil analysis. Nice job."

"Thanks. Do you have any questions?"

"Not really, but I did notice that anomaly you found with the soil from the clothes. It didn't quite match the surrounding dirt. Any ideas why?"

"Can't come up with one, Mo," Dr. Byrd replied. "But given the age and the immersion, I can only guess the original difference was a lot bigger."

"What do you mean?"

"If we can still find some differences in the chemical make-up after all these years, it must have been really pronounced back then. I'd guess the original dirt surrounding the body came from someplace completely separate from the lake or the shore."

"I can tell you this, though," he continued, "that boat had old lead-based paint. I don't think it's been used since the sixties. So the boat is older than our mystery."

"Can you trace it?" Driscoll asked.

"Not a chance, kid. Sorry."

"That's okay. Thanks for everything, Birdie."

"You still owe me that dinner, you know."

Driscoll hung up. She opened another file and called Gerry Peterson in Cherokee County. He'd sent the biggest report, with details on a dozen or so different samples and various tests. He must have had a lot of fun with his new toy, Driscoll thought.

"Good morning, Mo," Gerry said when he picked up. "Did you get my latest reports?"

"Just finished reading them," Driscoll replied. "That's why I'm calling."

"Where would you like to start?"

"I just got off the phone with Stuart Byrd and his soil analysis shows some weird readings. Did you see the same thing?"

"Sure did, and I think I know why. I'd say the dirt from the clothes and body was packed tight, so it didn't wash away completely."

"And if you've got some samples from around the area," he continued, "I might be able to match where this came from."

"Not from that long ago," Driscoll said. "But I could probably come up with some current ones. What am I looking for?"

"Lower phosphate and silicon content, higher nitrogen and a different mix of the usual suspects like sulfur, iron and the like."

"I'll see what I can find," Driscoll said. "Anything else really stand out, that's not in your report?"

"Did you look at the ink analysis?"

Driscoll's autopsy found stained skin remnants on one arm. All those years buried in the dirt and immersed in cold water left some soft tissue on the body. The state lab didn't identify it.

"I glanced at it. Can you tell me more?"

"It's a tattoo, if you hadn't guessed," Peterson said, "But that's not the interesting part. The ink isn't from this country and the method is old school, probably mid-sixties."

"How do you know that?"

"If you look at the skin under the microscope, you'll see the needle holes aren't exact along the edges and lines. This means the artist didn't use the electric gun they do now. The tat was done completely by hand."

"I bet that hurt."

"I wouldn't recommend it to anyone," Peterson said, "No matter how much they want some ink."

While her colleague described the tattoo, Driscoll reread the details on the ink itself.

"Gerry, you said the ink wasn't from here. Do you know where it came from?"

"Vietnam," Peterson replied. "Da Nang or Hue, if I had to guess."

"Good lord," Driscoll exclaimed. "How do you know that?"

"Hey kid, my new mass-spec can break stuff down all the way to the basic elements and then some. I found things you won't find anywhere but Southeast Asia, and mostly in the middle part of 'Nam. Besides, tattoo artists are rather finicky and a lot of them mix their own ink. I googled the ingredients and learned it's still used over there."

"Wow," Driscoll said, "that's impressive."

"Does it get me invited to dinner?"

"It does," she replied, cringing at what this would do to her expense report.

"Great," Gerry said. "I'll take my steak medium-well."

They rang off.

As Driscoll compiled all this information into a final detailed report, her phone rang.

"How's it going, sister?" Dr. Lois Lindlay said.

"Good, Lois, how are you?" Driscoll said. "Have you got something on the face mold?"

"Kinda, sorta," Lindlay replied. "That's why I'm calling. Would you mind some company for a few days?"

"Of course not," Driscoll replied. "But what's up? Couldn't your team re-create my victim's face?"

"Not really, Mo. But let's save it until I get there. I've got two lectures tomorrow, so how's Wednesday?"

"It works for me."

"Great," Dr. Lindlay said before hanging up. "And have the skull ready. We're going to need it."

***

Tuesday passed quietly for Corey and Michelle. The weekend's excitement faded and classes returned to normal. As they left the last class, Mr. Isaacs asked how their research on the old ring was going.

"Slow," Corey said. "We've found some possible names, but haven't had time to check into them."

"We're also helping Officer Shelton identify the dead body we found," Michelle added.

"I know," Isaacs replied, "and she appreciates it. But what exactly are you doing about the ring? Have you checked the Naval Academy website?"

Corey and Michelle looked at each other.

"Mr. Geltsin at the paper suggested that too," Corey said, "but we hadn't tried yet."

"Would they have records from that far back?" Michelle asked.

"Easy enough to find out," Isaacs replied. "But even if they don't, there are other resources. Use your imagination."

"Thanks, Mr. Isaacs," Corey said.

As they waited for Brenda Shelton outside the paper's old office, the kids talked about websites and other places to look for the ring's owner.

"I bet we'll find a lot of possible names on that website," Corey said. "This may be easy after all."

"Maybe not, Corey," Michelle said, "If they don't have records from the sixties online, we might be back where we started."

"I know, but searching the Web will be faster than searching old files."

"What are you searching the Web for?" Officer Shelton asked as she walked up. She unlocked the door and they entered the dark office.

"The owner of the ring Corey found," Michelle said. "Mr. Geltsin told us to search the Naval Academy website."

"Mr. Isaacs suggested it too," Corey added.

"Good idea," Shelton said, "but let's work on finding the dead guy first. How long can you stay?"

"Until my mom calls," Corey said. "She's our ride home."

"I've got 'til six, then I have to report for duty."

Shelton and the kids went downstairs and dropped their things on the work table. Papers from nineteen seventy-two were already stacked there, so they split the issues and went to work.

"What exactly are we searching for?" Michelle asked.

"Check the police calls for anything from the lake or any report of someone missing," Shelton said.

They worked quietly for thirty minutes, making it through the entire year, but found nothing of interest. Corey helped the officer put the papers back on the shelf and grab nineteen seventy-one. Again, they split the issues.

"This might be something," Michelle said, pointing to the paper she was looking through.

"What is it?" Shelton asked.

"A report of two stolen boats up at the lake." She passed the paper over to the officer.

"Two boats were stolen from Hempley's Rental," Michelle explained for Corey. "They're described as light blue with white trim."

"That's the color of the boat we found on the lake's bottom," Corey said.

"Unfortunately, that's about all it says," Shelton said. "But it might be something. At least it's a timeframe."

Silence returned as they continued reading.

"I don't think I want to meet this guy," Corey said after more minutes reading. "He seems to get arrested every few weeks. Mostly for fighting,"

"What are you talking about?" Michelle asked.

"I'm working from January forward," Corey said, "and it seems like every three or four weeks, this Pete Simpkins was arrested for assault or fighting or something."

"I saw his name too," Shelton said. "In fact, I think there was a front-page story with that name." She flipped back through the issues from summer.

"Here," she said. "A story about Pete Simpkins being tried for assault and rape."

"Was he convicted?" Michelle asked.

"No he wasn't," Shelton said. "He was acquitted on both charges."

Corey's phone buzzed at five forty-five. He read the message.

"That was my mom," he said. "Time to go home."

"Go ahead, you two," Shelton said. "I'll finish and lock up."

"When do you want help again?" Michelle asked.

"Tomorrow would be great," Shelton replied, "and at this rate, we'll probably finish it up then. I don't think we'll have any luck past nineteen sixty-nine."

"I'll have to talk to my mom," Michelle said. "She's supposed to take us home tomorrow."

They did make it all the way through nineteen sixty-nine and seventy the next evening. Pete Simpkins came up a few more times in nineteen seventy, but they didn't find any stories or mentions of missing people.

"Well, I guess this was a dead end," Shelton said as the kids stacked the last papers. "But it was worth checking."

"What will you do next?" Michelle asked.

"I'll put together a report and give it to the detectives. I know we didn't find any real clue, but this is still information. It may prove something."

"Will you keep working on it?" Corey asked.

"Sure," Shelton said. "At least I'll keep trying."

They said goodbye as Corey and Michelle headed over to the courthouse. Mrs. Pritchard picked them up there.

After finishing their homework that night, both kids worked on their computers to find anything they could on the old ring. Corey quickly navigated to the Academy's website and found the link to the Alumni Association. From there, however, he couldn't find a class listing. Corey found most information was protected and only available to other graduates and families, He did write down the contact information.

Michelle found a Wikipedia list for Naval Academy grads, but it only told her about notable people. Whoever they were looking for wouldn't be on this.

"Have any luck?" she asked Corey the next day at school.

"No, but I did write down who we can contact. We might need to do this the old fashioned way."

"Do you think they'll answer a letter or email from two kids?"

"I don't know why not, since we're trying to locate the person who owns that ring and return it."

"Yeah, but we might have better luck if we could make it a little more official."

They each thought for a few seconds.

"Here's an idea," Michelle said. "Officer Shelton."

"Here's a better one," Corey said. "Judge Danielson."

"You're right," Michelle said. "That is a better one."

After school, they went to the courthouse and asked the judge if he would help contact the Naval Academy. He not only agreed, but told the kids he'd get in touch with a high school friend who went on to Annapolis.

"He'll know exactly who and how to ask," Danielson said.

"Do you think he'll come up with something?" Corey asked.

"Probably," Danielson said, "If there's something to find. But it might take a while, so don't expect an immediate answer."

"We won't, sir," Michelle said.

"Okay. Give me all the details you have, and I'll contact my friend."

Corey wrote down everything they knew, from how he stumbled over the ring to how they cleaned it up and the information he got from Mr. Jason at the mall. He sent it to Michelle to clean up and she rewrote his notes as a letter. They included pictures and Annette took the package to Judge Danielson the next morning.

Chapter XIII

Dr. Lois Lindlay walked into the Wagner County morgue carrying her laptop in a shoulder bag and wheeling two hard-sided cases. She put down her gear next to Driscoll's desk.

"How's it going, girl?" she asked as her friend stood. They hugged.

"Going well," Driscoll said. "So what did you bring me?"

"Just myself, my expertise, and a 3-D scanner I guarantee will make you jealous."

"That's mean, Lois," Driscoll said, laughing.

Dr. Lindlay set up the scanner on an empty examining table. Dr. Driscoll retrieved the cleaned skull from its storage drawer and placed it in the scanner's chamber. Lindlay brought up her laptop and started the scan program.

"How does this work?" Driscoll asked.

"Lasers first create a grid pattern and then fill in the spots where there's something solid. Sort of like a radar photograph, but with several factors more exact detail."

"You lost me at lasers, Lois."

Dr. Lindlay laughed. "The thing does have that effect."

"How long will it take?" Driscoll asked.

"The scan will take most of the morning," Lindlay said. "Then my re-creation program will need two or three hours to develop a face to go with it."

"That long? I thought it would be quicker."

"This isn't TV, Mo," Dr. Lindlay said. "These things take time."

She checked to make sure things were running well. "Okay, now that it's going, what else can you tell me about the deceased?"

Driscoll took out her growing files and notes. While her friend read the reports, Driscoll did paperwork. The two women were quiet for almost an hour.

"Lots of good detail, Mo," Lindlay said after closing the last folder. "But there isn't anything tying it all together."

"I know," Driscoll replied. "That's where I'm hoping you can help. Maybe a face will give the police a place to start."

Lindlay's computer beeped. "The scan's finished."

Dr. Lindlay hit some keys on her computer. "Okay, I've got the basic information, now I need to compile it into a rendering of the skull."

"How long will that take?" Driscoll asked.

"Long enough to pack up the scanner, grab some lunch, and start catching up."

After sandwiches at Hickman's, the two doctors returned to the lab. Lindlay's computer program was ready to create a facial profile and they started the process.

"Again, we wait," Dr. Lindlay said.

"How long now?" Driscoll asked.

"Most of the afternoon, and maybe into tonight. That's why I brought my overnight bag."

Driscoll laughed. "And I thought you just wanted some time away from your office and the chance to catch up."

"That too, Mo, but the thing does take time."

As the computer worked, the women talked, telling stories, catching up on their own lives, along with what they'd heard about friends and colleagues.

"You need to meet my counterparts in Cherokee and Morris counties," Driscoll said. "You'd enjoy them."

"Are they single?" Lindlay asked.

"Birdie is," Driscoll chuckled. "But Gerry's well married with three little kids."

"Speaking of kids, Mo," Lindlay said, "what's the deal with those two who found your body? Seems to be a habit."

"I know," Driscoll replied, "but they're good kids and really curious. I'm not surprised they're involved in this."

Dr. Lindlay's program showed just over halfway complete by five o'clock, so the women wrapped things up and headed out. They went to dinner at Clayton's and continued catching up.

The next morning, the re-creation program showed complete and Lindlay displayed the face for Driscoll.

"Looks pretty average," Driscoll said.

"True, but it's something," Lindlay replied. "The nose and mouth are distinctive, and the hairline's something to go on, too."

"But I still don't recognize him."

"Good lord, Mo," Lindlay said. "The body was in the lake for over forty years. How would you recognize him?"

"You're right," Driscoll said. "And I guess we've done as much as we can here. I'll send the rendering over to the police and sheriff with copies of all my other results."

"Glad I could help."

As Lindlay packed her laptop, Driscoll's phone rang. She said hello and listened for several seconds.

"What can I do to help?" she asked and then listened for more seconds.

"Okay, Birdie," she said. "I'll get ready here and send my team."

"What's going on?" Lindlay asked after Driscoll hung up.

"There's been a major accident over in Morris County," Dr. Driscoll replied. "A van missed a curve and crashed upside down in Jewel Creek. Four dead and another four injured."

"So they need your help?"

"Dr. Byrd and I always cover each other, and the creek's the county line." She picked up the phone.

"Sarah," she said, "grab Tyler and Davis, and get all three wagons ready. Tell John to prep here for at least three bodies."

"You want to help, Lois?" she asked after hanging up again.

"I've never worked a crime scene and haven't done an autopsy since residency. I don't think I'd be much use, Mo."

"Sure you would," Driscoll said, "and I'll take all the help I can get."

Lindlay put her computer and other things in her car and joined Driscoll in the ME's wagon. Processing the scene and gathering and transporting the victims took the rest of the morning. The post-mortems and full autopsies extended through the afternoon and evening, so Dr. Lindlay spent another night with Dr. Driscoll. She headed back to the university the next morning.

***

After giving their materials to Judge Danielson, Corey and Michelle didn't know where to look next. The only new information they'd come up with was from helping Officer Shelton look through the old newspapers. No clues there, but Corey wondered if there was a connection.

"Hey Shel," he said as they sat in the courthouse break room. "Do you think the dead guy actually owned the ring? Maybe we need to start looking for who he was."

"We can't do that," Michelle said. "It's a real case. You know what the sheriff told us. We can't get involved."

"But we already are," Corey replied. "We found the body, and we've been helping Officer Shelton do research. I bet she'd let us look closer."

"Let us look closer at what?" Michelle asked. "The case files?"

"Sure," Corey said. "We've done it before and maybe there's some new information by now. At least we can ask."

"Okay, we can ask." Michelle took out her phone and dialed Shelton. She left a message when the officer didn't pick up, asking if she and Corey could look at any new information on the dead man.

"I guess we wait some more," Michelle said after ending the call.

With the accident and the usual happenings around the county, two days passed before Detectives Ruter and Harding received Driscoll's reports. Officer Shelton received a copy, too, and spent an evening reading through everything.

Before her shift the next day, Shelton walked over to the sheriff's office and found Detective Harding at his desk. She knew Ruter would be along soon.

"Have you read through Dr. Driscoll's reports?" Shelton asked.

"Sure have," Harding replied. "What about them?"

"Well, there's a lot of new information, and I've come up with some things on my own," Shelton said, "so I was thinking we should sit down and go over everything, to see where we go next."

"There's nowhere to go," Harding said. "Yes, the ME came up with a lot of new details, but there's nothing to tie anything together."

"What about the facial reconstruction?" Shelton said. "That's something. Maybe somebody will recognize the man."

"What do you want us to do?" Harding said. "Put up wanted posters? Or maybe put his face on milk cartons."

"Not bad ideas, Bobby," Detective Ruter said as he walked up. "Someone might actually recognize him."

"Thank you, Detective," Shelton said.

"Don't thank me yet, Brenda," Ruter said. "Bobby's right. There's nothing to go on. There's a lot of information here, but that's all it is. If you had something to point us in one direction, we might be able to figure this out."

"I've got some ideas, and I found some things in the old papers," Shelton said.

"So go work on them," Harding said, "and let us do our own jobs."

The detective picked up a file, ending the conversation. Shelton walked away angrily.

Back at her own desk, she came up with an idea. If the sheriff's detectives wouldn't help identify the dead man, she'd go at it another way. She picked up her phone and dialed.

"Rich Geltsin," the editor of the *Record / Times* said, picking up.

"Mr. Geltsin, this is Brenda Shelton. Can we meet?"

"Have you got something for me, Officer?"

"More like a request, though I think you will get a story out of it."

They arranged to meet at the old office the next afternoon.

After ending the call, Shelton saw the older message from Michelle. She listened to it and another idea formed. She returned the call.

"Hi, Michelle, this is Brenda Shelton."

"Hi, Officer Shelton," Michelle replied. "Is anything wrong?"

"No, I'm returning your call. Are you and Corey still interested in helping me?"

"Sure, but we don't know what to do next."

"That's okay, I've got some ideas. Can you two come down to the old *Record / Times* office tomorrow after school?"

Michelle thought for a moment. "I think so. Corey's mom is supposed to pick us up and we can ask her to bring us down to the courthouse instead of dropping us at home."

"Great," Shelton said. "I'll see you about three-thirty. Bring all your notes too."

After getting Marybelle's permission to not come straight home, Michelle called Corey and set things up. Annette was happy to bring the kids downtown because she'd be away from the office for less time.

They all met on the sidewalk in front of the paper's building. Walking in, they found Rich Geltsin working at one of the desks and they each grabbed a chair and sat down.

"Hello, Brenda" the editor said. "Seeing these two with you really has me interested. What have you got?"

"Hi, Rich," Shelton said. "I've got a lot of information on that body the kids found, but nowhere to go. I thought I'd let you look at the reports—off the record, of course…"

"Of course," Geltsin said, smiling, "though I can easily get hold of them on the record."

"I know you can," Shelton said. "But this way we can see where things are headed, if anywhere."

She placed the stack of folders on the desk. Shelton hadn't brought the complete files, just the summaries and some supporting documents.

"Okay, I'll look these over," Geltsin said. "But is there anything you're holding back?"

Shelton smiled. "Yes, but it's in the top file. I wanted all of you to see it together."

He turned to Corey and Michelle. "And what about you two? What do you have for me?"

"We're still trying to find out about the old ring I found," Corey said.

"And we're wondering if it was the dead man's," Michelle added.

"We tried looking online like you said," Corey continued, "but couldn't find anything."

"So Judge Danielson said he'd make sort of an official request for us," Michelle said.

"But that's going to take time," Corey added, "and we want to keep trying while we wait."

"Okay, okay," Geltsin said. "Show me what you've learned, before I wear my neck out trying to keep up with you."

As the kids took their notes out and put them on the desk, Geltsin looked at Shelton.

"Do they do this to you, too?" he asked.

Officer Shelton smiled but didn't respond.

"We've got pictures from all angles," Michelle said "And Corey had Mr. Jason at the mall look at it. He found the initials on the inside."

"So you really don't have much, do you?" Geltsin said.

"Not really," Corey said. "But it might be connected to the body."

"Alright, let's see what we've got." Geltsin opened the top folder and looked at what Dr. Lindlay's program had created for the dead man's face.

Officer Shelton gave copies of her files to Corey and Michelle, too. The group spent several minutes silently reading until Corey spoke.

"Hey, Shel, look at this," he said, showing one of the ME's reports to Michelle.

"What is it?"

"A metal ID tag they found on the boat."

"Remember when we were searching the old papers," Corey continued, "and I found that thing about missing rental boats?"

"I remember," Michelle said, "What about it?"

Geltsin and Shelton looked up.

"Those boats were the same color," Corey said, "Maybe this ID tag could prove where the boat we found came from."

"When was that story printed, Corey?" Geltsin asked.

"Nineteen seventy-one, I think," Corey replied. "I don't remember exactly but it was around the middle of our helping you."

"I think you're right," Shelton said. "I remember your mentioning it, and I think the article said the boats went missing from Hempley's."

"Aren't they still renting boats at the lake?" Michelle asked.

"They are," Geltsin said. "It's a family business. Jed runs it these days. His dad, Willie, is retired mostly, though he does some farming at their old place."

"Why don't Michelle and I go check it out?" Corey said. "This could be a real clue."

"Hold on, Corey," Shelton said, "Don't go snooping around up there on your own. Let's do this right. If Mr. Hempley was involved somehow, I'll check it out."

"And I'll find that story downstairs if needed," Geltsin said, making notes.

The group continued reading silently.

"Okay," Geltsin said, closing his last folder. "We've got a body in the lake for over forty years, foul play likely, a tattoo from Vietnam and now a potential face to go with everything. There just might be a story here."

"Don't forget the ring," Michelle said.

"I didn't," Geltsin replied, "but we'll come back to it."

"Meantime," he continued, "there's no possible identification, no DNA or other trace, and basically no way to verify anything."

"And no interest from the sheriff's department to find out," Shelton said.

Geltsin looked at each face across the desk.

"Folks," he said after several seconds, "I believe we have a mystery. And if you're willing to keep at it with me, we just might be able to solve it."

"I'm in," Corey said.

"Me too," Michelle added.

"How about you, Brenda?" Geltsin asked.

"Yes, I'll help. But I just hope my boss doesn't object too much."

"I wouldn't worry about it," Geltsin said. "I doubt the chief will have a problem, as long as Sheriff Wingate doesn't."

He stacked all the materials and packed them up.

"By the way, I'm not sure the ring you two found will help us find out who the man was. It's an interesting story, but might not be connected."

"But it might be, right?" Corey asked.

"Yes, it might," Geltsin answered. "And anyway, the Naval Academy is a big deal, and even if it was a long time ago, I bet people remember someone who attended and graduated. It will be part of the story. Who knows? One mystery might lead to the other.

"Now I'm going to get to work. I can't say when the story will appear, so stay tuned."

"What can we do?" Corey asked.

"Right now, nothing," Geltsin said. "But if my story generates any new leads, I'll probably ask you to follow up. You can interview people."

On the way back to meet Annette at the courthouse, Corey told Michelle he wanted to check out their boat lead anyway.

"We could actually learn something new about this," he said, "instead of waiting for something to happen.

"No, Corey," Michelle said, "Officer Shelton said she'd check it out."

"Come on, Shel, we don't have to tell anyone. Besides, the place is probably deserted. Let's ride up there on Saturday and look around. What could happen?"

"We could get caught trespassing."

"Only if someone spots us."

"Okay, okay," Michelle said. "But if someone's there, we leave."

The weather as still warm for autumn, so Corey and Michelle only needed light jackets as they pedaled up to Lake Cyrus. Hempley's Boats & Bait looked deserted as the two friends parked their bikes next to a tree. Rental boats were leaned upside down on old railroad ties. Like the boat they'd found down in the mud, all were light blue with white trim.

"We need to check for ID tags," Corey said. "The report said it was under the rim lip."

"I know," Michelle replied, "but let's make it fast. Okay?"

Corey ran his fingers under the curled rim of the first boat. He hit something just before the bow end. It felt metal to him and he tried to look at whatever it was.

"I think there's a tag here," he said, "But I can't see it."

"What are you two doing there?" A voice from behind them said. Both kids jumped at the sound and turned. A forty-ish man in jeans and a denim shirt walked toward them from the main building.

"I don't think you'll find much use for a boat today, unless you want to drag it all the way to the river.

"Umm, hi," Corey said, still startled. "Are you Mr. Hempley?"

"I guess," the man said. "I'm Jed Hempley. Most folks call my dad Mr. Hempley."

"I'm Michelle Pritchard," Michelle said, "And this is Corey Palmer."

"It's nice to meet you," Jed Hempley said. "But I've got to ask you again, what are you doing?"

"We think we found one of your boats," Corey said.

"I don't think so, son," Jed replied, shaking his head. "All of our boats are accounted for."

"This one was at the bottom of the lake," Michelle said.

"We found it when we were exploring down there," Corey added, "It was down there for a long time."

"Are you kids serious?" Jed asked.

"Yessir," Michelle said. "There was even a..."

Corey nudged Michelle to cut her off.

"There was even a metal ID tag on the boat," Corey said, taking the picture of the tag out of his pocket.

Jed looked at the picture. "Holy Jesus," he said, "That does look like one of ours. But it's really old."

"It was down there a long time," Michelle said.

"And we found an old article in the paper about a couple of your boats missing," Corey added, "when we were looking for information on something else."

"That's strange," Jed said, "We've never had any boats turn up missing as long as I've worked here."

"The paper was from nineteen seventy-one," Corey said.

"You're kidding me," Jed said, laughing.

"No, sir," Michelle said. She and Corey explained how they jumped into the mud and then explored the lake bottom, discovering the boat. They didn't mention the dead man.

"I don't believe it," Jed said. He turned toward the building.

"Hey, Pop," he called, "Come on out. You gotta hear this story."

A gray-haired man in a checked shirt, jeans, and a ball cap, walked out of the building and joined the group.

"Kids, this is my dad, Willie Hempley," Jed said.

"Hi, I'm Corey Palmer."

"I'm Michelle Pritchard."

"Fine," Willie Hempley said. "What's this story I need to hear."

"Well, sir," Corey said, "Michelle and I were exploring the lake after they drained it and we found an old boat we think might have been yours."

"It was the same color as yours and there was a metal tag underneath the rim," Michelle added.

Corey showed Willie Hempley the picture of the ID tag.

"We also read in the *Record / Times* where you reported some missing boats back in nineteen seventy-one," he said.

Willie looked at the picture, and then looked at the kids.

"I think you two need to mind your business," he said. "And I think you'd best get out of here. Go on." He turned to walk back inside.

"Pop, what's wrong?" Jed asked.

"Nothing, boy," the older man replied, "nothing. Just an old boat finally turning up."

He turned back to the others.

"I mean it, you two," he said, pointing his finger at Corey and Michelle. "Keep away from here and mind your own business. Now, git!"

Willie stomped back inside.

"I suppose he's right," Jed said. "Sorry we couldn't help." He turned to go inside too.

"Wow," Corey said, after the kids were alone. "I wonder what that's about."

"I don't know," Michelle said, "but maybe we should get out of here."

"Yeah, but we need to let someone know," Corey said, taking out his phone. "This could be important."

"You're not calling Officer Shelton, are you?" Michelle asked. "She told us not to come up here."

"Don't worry. I'm calling Mr. Geltsin. He didn't tell us not to check this out."

Chapter XIV

Rich Geltsin still had a newspaper to run, so the story took time to develop. He read through all the files, following up with Shelton and Dr. Driscoll for additional details, and asked Judge Danielson for updates on his request for information from Annapolis.

The story led the front page on Monday before Thanksgiving. The reconstructed face appeared to the left of the story's lead.

Do You Know This Man?

By Rich Geltsin
Editor

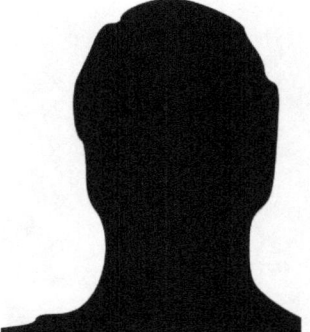

September's grisly find at the bottom of Lake Cyrus now has a face.

Wagner County Medical Examiner, Dr. Maureen Driscoll, released this re-creation of the deceased, after working with Dr. Lois Lindlay from the state university.

Dr. Driscoll stated this rendering

is probably the most accurate rendering possible, based on the condition of the remains discovered by two Craigsville youths.

Additional tests were performed by the medical examiner's office, but no details are being released yet. According to the Wagner County Sheriff's office and the Craigsville Police Department, there is not yet enough information to pursue a more active investigation.

The story went on to recount how Corey and Michelle found the body in the empty lake, the steps taken so far to determine who the man was, and describe the corpse's head injury and the tattoo. Toward the end, Geltsin finished by asking for help.

Community's Help Needed

Whoever this man was, he deserves his identity and his family deserves closure. Please help if you have any information.
Anyone knowing who this mystery man was is urged to contact the Wagner County Sheriff's Office, the Craigsville Police Department or the <u>Record / Times.</u>

At the bottom of page one, Geltsin included a short piece on the old ring.

Artifact Found In Lake

Human remains haven't been the only things found in the exposed Lake Cyrus mud recently. The lakebed also recently revealed another relic.

Corey Palmer and Michelle Pritchard, the two young people who discovered the body of the mystery man, also reported finding a class ring from the United States Naval Academy.

The ring, from the graduating class on 1965, was intact though missing the icon usually mounted on the gemstone. Initials were discovered on the inside of the ring, though it isn't clear if these are the owner's.

Anyone knowing of an Academy graduate from this era is encouraged to contact the Record / Times.

Older residents in the area quickly began talking about the mystery man. At a fast food restaurant by the highway, a group of coffee and breakfast regulars talked about it that morning. Rich Geltsin heard part of their conversation as he stood in line for his morning order.

"I could swear I should know this guy."

"You're getting old, Harry, and memory's the first thing to go."

"Don't get on him too bad, John, he's right—I think I know the man too. I think his name was Pete something."

"Right. Pete Simpson, I think."

"Not Simpson, Simpkins."

Two of the men were old pressmen from the paper, so Geltsin knew he could join the group. After paying for his food, he called his deputy editor and told her to handle the morning meeting. He was chasing a story.

"Okay, guys," he said as he sat down. "Talk to me. Tell me about this person."

Downtown at Hickman's Diner, another regular morning group was sure about the man in the paper.

"Yes, that's Pete Simpkins. I remember him."

"Me too. He was a bad dude."

"Uh-huh, always picking fights and messing with people. Looks like it finally caught up with him."

"Don't mean to speak ill, but it couldn't happen to a nicer fellow."

"I wonder if anyone's told Willie Hempley. Didn't Simpkins work for them out at the lake?"

"Yep, and Willie was just about the only friend Simpkins had."

Chief Judge Howard Barker listened to this conversation as he finished his breakfast. He remembered Pete Simpkins quite well. After paying for his meal, he walked to the courthouse lost in the memory of his first trial as a prosecutor over forty years earlier.

The other judges began talking about the article after concluding business in their weekly conference.

"I've already had a couple of old-timers tell me the man's name was Simpkins," Judge MacGruder said, "But it's before my time."

"I think it's pretty much before all our time," Judge Cohen added.

"That's true," Judge Rollins added, "but if something new is discovered, it might become our problem. There's no statute of limitations on murder."

"I think you're getting ahead of things," Judge Danielson said. "Even if people think they know who this man was, it's not confirmed and his death might not have been a homicide. And there are certainly no suspects if it was."

"Theo, wasn't it your clerk's son and his friend who found the body?" Judge Sims asked.

"Yes it was."

"So what else do you know? We all remember how you helped those kids figure out who the boy in the clock tower was. I'd bet they're working on this too."

"I don't have to say, Don," Judge Danielson replied, smiling. The other judges laughed.

Judge Barker hadn't said anything about the dead man or the newspaper article. Judge MacGruder noticed and asked the chief judge what he thought.

"I think I'd rather forget about the late Mr. Simpkins," Barker replied, "if that's who he was."

"Do you remember the man?" Judge Rollins asked.

"Unfortunately, I do. And it's not something I'm proud of."

"Tell us about it," Judge Cohen said. The others nodded agreement.

"Alright," Judge Barker said, "here's the story. Pete Simpkins was a bad one all around. He wasn't from around here, just showed up one day and started making trouble right off. Hardly a month went by that he didn't appear in one courtroom or another for drunkenness, fighting, or some type of disturbance. But then he was charged with assault and rape.

"Who was the victim?" Danielson asked.

"Clara Wingate."

"As in Sheriff Wingate?" MacGruder asked.

"Indeed," Barker said, "though she was Clara Abel then."

"Anyway," Barker continued, "I was brand new as the assistant prosecutor, and this was my first trial here. Simpkins and Clara got together at that old joint by the Cooper mill and apparently after some drinks, they left. She said he took her up to the lake and roughed her up, then raped her. She reported it and he was arrested."

"Did you get a conviction?" Judge Sims asked.

"No I didn't. I thought we had a good case, but his lawyer ripped poor Clara up on the stand and the jury ended up thinking she'd led him on."

"You're kidding!" Judge Rollins exclaimed. "That's ridiculous!"

"It was the early seventies," Barker said. "Different times."

"I hope he at least straightened up afterwards," Rollins said.

"He didn't. He bragged about it and kept acting up."

"Where was Mort Wingate during this?" Judge Cohen asked.

"He was serving in Vietnam," Barker said. "He didn't come home until later that year. I don't think he ever knew what happened."

***

As she did every day, Annette neatly stacked Judge Danielson's mail and set it on his desk that morning. She didn't open things addressed directly to the judge, particularly not things labeled "confidential" like the large envelope delivered that day. She didn't notice the return address, United States Naval Academy Alumni Foundation.

Judge Danielson worked his way through the mail, reading and noting items requiring rerouting or further information. He came to the large envelope last. Opening it, he took out a manila folder

containing several pages, starting with a letter.

The Honorable Theodore J. Danielson
Wagner County Superior Court
2 West Main Street
Craigsville, ___ 39999

Dear Judge Danielson:

Regarding your request for information on the owner of a USNA class ring, we are happy to provide what facts we can. With the help of your pictures and other details, we were able to search the records for the Class of 1965, and did find one midshipman with the initials inscribed on the inside of the ring.

Paul Malcolm Strickland entered the US Naval Academy during the summer term of 1961, and graduated with his class in the spring of 1965. As such, he would have been entitled to wear the ring you discovered and since no other midshipman in that class had the same initials, it is very likely you are in possession of Strickland's ring.

However, records show that while Midshipman Strickland did graduate and was commissioned as an officer in the United States Navy, Lt. (j.g.) Paul Strickland was reported shot down over North Vietnam in March of 1969, while flying his F-4 Phantom off the USS Enterprise as a member of VF116.

Neither his body nor the wreckage of his plane was ever discovered, and he is officially listed as MIA-presumed dead.

There is no way of knowing how you and your friends came into possession of Lt. Strickland's ring, and as we have no record of any living family, you are free to do with it as you see fit.

We are enclosing a picture of Lt. Strickland, along with a summary of what records the Alumni Foundation has. We sincerely hope you might find this information useful.

Best regards,

Howard D. Lashbrook Cmdr. USN (Ret.)
Coordinator, Class of 1965

Judge Danielson put the letter aside looked at the other materials. Looking at the picture, he immediately saw a stark resemblance to the re-creation of the man Corey and Michelle found in Lake Cyrus.

"My lord," he thought. He called Annette into his office.

"Can you call or text Corey to come by here after school," he asked, "Along with Miss Pritchard?"

"Certainly, Judge," Annette said. "What's it about?"

"I received a reply from the Naval Academy, and I want to share it," the judge replied. "I'd also like to hear what they've learned."

"And I think they will be very surprised."

Corey read Annette's text as he and his friends left the cafeteria after lunch.

"Cool," he said. "The judge got an answer. He wants to share it with us after school."

"An answer to what?" Tim Crane asked.

"He had a friend ask the Naval Academy to find the owner of that class ring," Michelle said.

"And we're hoping they found something," Corey said.

"Do you think it might be the man in the paper?" Paula Terrill asked.

"I don't know," Michelle said. "It's possible, I guess."

"I wonder if they'll ever find out who he really was," Paula said.

"Maybe it's another Cooper," Tim said as they passed a group of older boys in the hall. "They tend to disappear like that, and you two are really good at finding their rotten and nasty remains."

Tommy Cooper heard this and turned angrily.

"Shut up, Crane," he said, grabbing Tim's arm and pushing him against the wall. "You don't talk about my family like that."

"Take it easy, Cooper," Corey said. "He was joking."

Tommy turned. "Stay out of this, Palmer, it's between me and Crane here."

"He's right, man," Tim said hoarsely, as he struggled against Tommy's arm. "I was joking."

"Stop it, Tommy," Michelle said. "We aren't going to fight. We've had enough of that."

Tommy stepped back, releasing Tim from the wall. "Just watch your mouth. You know what can happen to you."

"And Mikey knows what can happen to you," Michelle said. Mike Baxter cringed slightly.

"You're not worried the dead man really *is* another relative of yours, are you?" Paula asked.

"Do you know something we don't, Cooper?" Corey asked. "Something you're not telling us?"

"Don't be stupid," Tommy said as he and his friends walked away.

"Wow," Tim said. "I'd say we got lucky there."

"Dumb luck," Paula said. "You shouldn't have snarked at him in the first place, Tim. We don't need another round with those jerks."

***

Judge Danielson met them next to Annette's desk after school. Grabbing sodas for everyone, he ushered the kids into his office and closed the door.

"Do you want me to tell you, or would you like to read it yourself?" he asked Corey and Michelle.

"Let's just read it," Corey said.

The judge passed the file over. Corey opened it and he and Michelle read the letter, then turned to the picture and other papers.

"*Oh My God!*" Michelle exclaimed. "That's the same man as in the paper this morning!"

"It does look that way," Danielson said.

"This says his name was Paul Strickland," Corey said, "but also says he disappeared in nineteen sixty-nine. How can it be the same person?"

"And how could he end up in the lake?" Michelle asked.

"That would seem to be the question," Danielson said. "Any ideas?"

Before either of them could answer, raised voices came from outside the office.

"Ma'am, you can't barge in there," they heard Annette say.

"Watch me," came the reply. The door opened and Brenda Shelton strode in.

"I knew I'd find both offenders here. Thank you, Your Honor, for having them already in custody. It will save me rounding them up."

"Officer Shelton, what's this about?" Danielson said.

"It's about obstruction, impeding an investigation and disobeying a police officer," Shelton replied. "Take your pick."

"What is she talking about, Corey?" Annette asked as she followed the officer in.

"Umm, well Mom..." he stammered. "We were just trying to..." Michelle punched his shoulder, silencing him.

"Didn't I tell you NOT to go up to Hempley's place at the lake?" Shelton asked sternly. Neither of the kids said anything.

"Well?"

"Yes, ma'am, you did," Michelle said, quietly.

"We were just following up on some new information," Corey added, "trying to learn things."

"Well you've certainly learned how to raise a stink," Shelton said. "First, you go up there snooping around, and then you called Rich Geltsin at the paper, instead of me.

"And so he calls Detective Ruter for confirmation, who doesn't know what's going on, which means Geltsin goes to the sheriff for answers. In the meantime, Willie Hempley calls Sheriff Wingate directly, complaining he's being harassed by two brats.

"So then the sheriff realizes it's my investigation into the dead body you found causing this uproar, and he calls Chief Blaise who brings me in for an explanation."

Shelton took a breath. "And that's what I want—an explanation. Why did you two go up there poking around after I told you specifically not to? What were you thinking?"

"Is this true, Corey?" Annette asked. "Did you disobey Officer Shelton?"

"Uh-huh," Corey replied. "But we were checking out the boats. We wanted to see if the boat we found was the same as the ones Mr. Hempley rents."

"We never said a word about the dead body," he continued.

"That's right," Michelle added. "We just thought that metal tag might match one on their boats."

"And did it?" Judge Danielson asked.

"That's not the point, Your Honor," Shelton said, "These two are interfering in an official investigation. They had no business going up there and could have gotten themselves in trouble."

"Wait a minute," Michelle said. "You asked us to help and we've been working hard on this."

"And we're also looking for different answers," Corey said, "We're trying to find who owned that old class ring."

"But now you've crossed the line," Shelton said. "You're in my territory. That ID tag and anything about the boat involves the dead man."

"But we're the ones who found out about the missing boats from the paper," Michelle said.

"And you wouldn't have made the connection without it," Corey added. "Or known to check out Mr. Hempley's place."

"That's not the point," Shelton said, but Judge Danielson cut her off.

"I think that is the point," he said, "or at least part of it."

Shelton turned to the judge.

"Officer Shelton," Danielson continued, "it seems these two have done you a favor. They checked out some information that you hadn't bothered with, and it seems they've caused a reaction. I think you might want to follow it up, rather than complaining about their actions."

"But, sir," Shelton said, "they're getting into things they shouldn't, and coming very close to violating the law."

"Well, they do seem to have that talent," Danielson replied, smiling. "But I think the only things Mr. Palmer and Miss Pritchard are guilty of are excessive curiosity, and maybe a lack of patience."

"But we do need to have a talk about listening to a police officer," Annette said. "Right, Corey?"

"Yes, Mom," Corey said.

"Alright, then," Danielson said. "Let's all start working together."

He gave the Naval Academy file to Shelton.

"And here's some new information," he said. "Thanks to Corey and Michelle, we might have a name to go with the face."

Shelton opened the file and saw the picture.

"My god, you're right!" She skimmed the rest of the information.

"Can I keep this?" she asked.

"No," the judge answered, "but I'll send copies to you and the detectives. Corey and Michelle get the original. After all, this is their mystery."

Danielson also sent a copy to Rich Geltsin.

Chapter XV

"Come on, Michelle," Marybelle called down the hallway. "It's nine-fifty and we have to leave by ten."

"Do we have to do this?" Michelle said as she walked into the kitchen.

"Yes, we have to do this," Marybelle replied. "It's important for our community, and you're old enough to help out. So quit complaining."

"Besides," Pete Pritchard said, looking up from his newspaper, "where else would we go? Everyone from church and most of your friends will be there too."

"We could be with Grandma, like we are at Christmas," Michelle said.

"Grandma's on a cruise," Marybelle pointed out.

"Well, I could stay here and work on the car with Daddy," Michelle said.

"And that would take care of about forty-five minutes," Pete said. "All I'm doing today is stripping and polishing the hubcaps."

"And what would you do after that? I have to get some sleep because I have a very early dispatch time. You'd end up doing nothing since I'll need quiet around here."

"And it could be worse," Marybelle said. "It could be our turn to clean up everything, like the Baptists this year."

"Alright," Michelle whined, "but I'm doing it under protest."

"No, you are not, young lady," Marybelle said sternly. "You will put on a smile, work hard, and have a good time. Are we clear?"

"And also," Pete said, "you do *not* want to miss out on Miss Eloise and her church ladies' cooking. If you don't do anything else, Shelly, bring me leftovers."

"I will, Daddy."

"Oh, and expect to be sort of a celebrity, too, sweetie," Pete said, folding the newspaper back to show the front page again.

"It looks like your digging into who that dead guy was is starting to pay off." He pointed to the lead article. "Take a look."

Michelle read the article.

Mystery Man Identified?

By Rich Geltsin
Editor

The mysterious body found in Lake Cyrus might now have a name, according to long-time area residents. Several people have identified the man as Pete Simpkins, who lived in the Craigsville area for two or three years back around 1970.

Dr. Maureen Driscoll, Wagner County Medical Examiner, confirmed the body was immersed in the lake for over forty years, and that the death was the result of foul play. While she could not establish an exact date of death, Dr. Driscoll stated more tests were still being conducted, including DNA analysis and soil samples from the area. The body was discovered earlier this year by Craigsville residents, Corey Palmer and Michelle Pritchard.

Residents recall Simpkins as not being native to the area, but just showing up in the one day. He is reported to have worked at Hempley's Boat & Bait Shop for a while, but this was not confirmed.

County records do show Pete Simpkins being arrested numerous times for offenses ranging from Drunk & Disorderly to fighting and vandalism. He served 30 days in the Wagner County jail for one incident.

He was also arrested and charged with assault and rape in 1971, but was acquitted at trial.

Both the Wagner County Sheriff's Office and the Craigsville Police Department are continuing to investigate the matter.

"But there's nothing about what we found out from the Naval Academy," Michelle said.

"Maybe Mr. Geltsin didn't think it was important," Pete said. "After all, you and Corey are looking into something different."

"And anyway," Marybelle said, "it's time to go."

Michelle and her mother arrived at the Craigsville Baptist Church within fifteen minutes. As they parked, Corey was carrying in some boxes from a truck parked close to the back door.

"Hi, Shel," he called.

"Hi, Corey, what are you carrying?"

"I think these are plastic forks and spoons. Can you grab a couple? There's still a lot to carry in."

Michelle took two boxes from the man on the truck and followed Corey into the Fellowship Hall. They placed their loads on a table at the side, near the kitchen entrance. People would grab plates and cutlery here, moving over to the serving tables next to the pass-throughs from the kitchen.

All the food was being prepared elsewhere and would come over by truck throughout the afternoon. Though serving wouldn't start until noon, there was a lot of activity both in the hall and in the kitchen where the Hidden Oaks Church people were getting ready to receive the first wave of dishes from Holcomb Road.

Twenty years earlier, Father Fred at St. Barnabas Catholic Church in Craigsville and Reverend Meyers over at the big Baptist church in Morris each decided to hold a Thanksgiving dinner for those who might not otherwise have one. Tripping over each other trying to tap the same resources for supplies and donations, they combined their efforts. Over the years, other area churches joined in and the event grew to cover several counties. Anyone was welcome to come and eat, with donations gratefully accepted to help cover the costs. It became an annual tradition for everyone to join together for food and fellowship.

Today, there was a steering committee to run the dinner, and each church was responsible for one part. This year, the Holcomb Road AME Church would cook the feast, and that meant the legendary Miss Eloise Bidwell was in charge. She was sure to cook up not only the traditional turkey, stuffing, potatoes and such, but also greens, yams, spareribs, okra and who knew what else.

Hidden Oaks Church, where the Palmers and Pritchards attended, were in charge of the serving line. This also included preparing a few hundred meals for delivery to several retirement communities and shut-ins around the Craigsville area. Meals for people in the surrounding counties would be packed and sent directly from the Holcomb Road kitchen.

Father Fred was retired now, but his church still took a large role every year. They had transportation this year, and they'd corralled every church bus in the area along with a third of Wagner County's school bus fleet. They would shuttle folks from Morris, Creek City, and Tyrone, along with delivering meals.

Craigsville Baptist was hosting this year, so those folks would clean up afterward insuring everything was put away where it belonged.

No desserts would be provided. They usually went to waste as everyone filled up during the feast. A few years earlier, Emmanuel Lutheran decided to host a second event on the following Sunday afternoon. This would be when everyone could fill up on cakes, cookies, pumpkin and pecan pies, and whatever else turned up.

After helping unpack and organize the cutlery, plates and cups, Corey and Michelle went to the kitchen. Annette told them to start laying out the serving utensils on the main table.

"Every spot is labeled, but check with Mrs. Porter on what dishes need what."

They grabbed the bin filled with tongs, large spoons and such, and went back to the main hall. While they placed the service items, they talked.

"Did you see the paper this morning?" Corey asked.

"Yeah," Michelle said, "but Mr. Geltsin didn't print anything about what we'd learned."

"I know, and I wonder what's up. What do you think, Shel?"

"I don't know—maybe he didn't get the information."

"Or maybe he doesn't think it's important enough."

"I guess we'll have to wait and see," Michelle said.

"No we don't," Corey said. "We can ask him. Let's call him tomorrow and find out."

There were around fifty people in line when the doors opened at noon. Most were just regular people from the area, looking for an easy Thanksgiving dinner and some good company. Several farming families from Jameson County came over together in a rickety van, and they were made welcome.

Service was buffet style with everyone helping themselves. Corey and Michelle kept busy restocking pans of vegetables and salads, along with replacing the serving utensils as they became so overused they needed cleaning. They weren't alone, with probably a dozen others doing the same work. Conversation hummed as people joined each other at the long tables or headed outside to eat in the courtyard.

Before they realized it, two hours went by.

"This is really hard," Michelle said. "I'm getting tired."

"Me too," Corey said, "but time is flying by."

"Yeah, but I could use a break. And something to eat," Michelle said. "Everything smells so good."

"Then now is a good time to do it," Mrs. Block said as she brought a refill on sweet potatoes out. "You've worked hard so far, so go ahead. But not too long, the buses from Creek City and Morris should get here in about thirty minutes."

The kids quickly filled plates of their own and went back to the kitchen to eat. Activity swirled around as new trays of food came in from the back door.

They didn't have to wait until the next day to ask the editor about the story. Rich Geltsin showed up a few minutes later to grab several plates of food to go. The kids put down their plates to help fill his order.

"These are for the guys printing tomorrow's edition," he said. "They're just starting work."

"But the rest of my team and I will be back soon," he continued. "We're done with tomorrow's edition."

"Can Michelle and I talk to you then?" Corey asked.

"Sure, but I need to go now so the guys can eat this while it's still warm."

Buses from other counties began showing up around two-thirty, as expected. Many of these folks were homeless or down on their luck, but there were a few who wanted a good dinner without having to drive over. That's how it went—everyone was welcomed.

Rich Geltsin made it back by three o'clock, along with his reporters and editorial team. They all filled plates and sat together at a long table. Corey and Michelle were still helping, so couldn't break away to talk to the editor until most of the Record / Times people finished and left.

When things slowed a bit, the kids walked over to where Geltsin sat, finishing his second helping of spareribs.

"Mr. Geltsin," Corey said, "we saw the article in the paper today."

"Did you like it?" Geltsin asked.

"Yes sir," Michelle said, "but we were wondering about something."

"We wondered why you didn't say anything about what we found out from the Naval Academy," Corey said.

"About the ring we found and who owned it," Michelle added.

"Well, kids," Geltsin said, inviting the two to sit with him. "Several reasons. First, I'm not sure it's part of this story. It could just as easily be something completely different. So I made a decision to leave it out and concentrate on what I'd found out about the dead man himself."

"Second," the editor continued, "even if your ring *is* part of the story, I didn't want to give everything away at one time. There might be more to this than any of us know yet."

"And third—I didn't get the information until after I'd written the story."

"Oh," Michelle said. "I understand, I think."

"Don't worry, you two," Geltsin said. "Your ring could still be a story, so keep digging."

"What about that ID tag we checked out," Corey said, "the one from the boat where the body was?"

"What are you talking about?" Geltsin asked.

"I left you a message," Corey said, "but you didn't reply."

"Didn't Officer Shelton tell you we went up to Hempley's to ask about it?" Michelle said.

"I seem to remember she told you not to."

"Yeah, but…" Corey said.

"I'll check it out," Geltsin said. "And I'm sorry I missed your call."

"But you two need to be careful. You don't want to get in the way."

"Okay, everyone," Annette called from the kitchen. "Last round is here. Time to start wrapping things up and feed ourselves."

Though the event officially ran until five, by four o'clock the crowd was mostly people who'd been working throughout the day. Shuttle drivers returned from their last trips to get fed, and Miss Eloise brought her team from Holcomb Road to eat and receive well-deserved congratulations on a fabulous meal. Members of the Baptist congregation also started arriving to eat before cleaning up.

People also packed leftovers and extra meals for those who couldn't be there. Marybelle loaded two containers with food for Pete.

As they stood behind the serving line, Corey and Michelle saw Jed Hempley come in. He asked for two meals to go, one for him and the other for his father.

"Should we ask him about the boat again?" Corey asked Michelle.

"I don't know," Michelle answered. "He might still be mad."

"Let's try," Corey said. "At least we can apologize if he is."

They went up to Jed.

"Hi, Mr. Hempley," Michelle said. "Could we ask you something?"

"I suppose," Jed replied. "But if it's about that boat, I don't know what I can tell you."

"We're just trying to find out what happened," Corey said. "And if the boat was one of yours."

"We think it's connected to what we found," Michelle added.

"But it was before my time," Jed said.

"Your father might know something," Corey said.

"I think he made it clear he didn't want to talk about it," Jed replied.

"Could you ask him?" Michelle said. "We're not trying to make trouble, but it's important."

"It could help solve a mystery," Corey said.

Jed thought for a few seconds. "Okay, I'll ask him again," he said, "but no promises. If he says no, you have to drop it."

"Okay," Corey said.

"Give me your email addresses so I can let you know."

Chapter XVI

Though essential services were fully staffed, most Craigsville and Wagner County offices closed for the entire four-day weekend. Schools were out until the following Monday, and some businesses took the days off too. Since the *Record / Times* didn't publish on the weekend, Rich Geltsin and his employees enjoyed a small break once the Friday edition was sent to press and the large advertising supplement created.

The medical examiner's office didn't close completely, but only one person was in the office, with everyone else on-call if needed. Tyler Graves drew the duty that Friday.

Mail delivery was normal and Tyler sorted through the day's items. Most he laid on Dr. Driscoll's desk, but some he routed to colleagues. He left the large envelope from a research lab upstate at the top of the pile. Dr. Driscoll was out of town until Sunday and not due back in the office until Monday, though available if needed.

Since the library and the courts were closed, Annette and Marybelle took off early to hit the mall and several big-box stores in search of bargains and gifts. They planned to shop through the morning, ending up back on the square to have lunch and then look through the downtown stores.

Corey and Michelle met Paula and Tim at his house. The Cranes attended Emmanuel Lutheran, so Tim's mom was up to her elbows baking brownies, cookies, and other treats for the Sunday get-together there. The kids spent a little time doing schoolwork, but mostly read or surfed the Web. Corey and Paula took a try at one of Tim's video games, but neither did well, though Paula did kill off Corey's character three times.

Mrs. Crane finally told them to get out after they'd stolen too many macadamia clusters and chocolate chip cookies. So the four headed downtown to check out what was happening.

Craigsville's main square was busy with shoppers and visitors filling the sidewalks. Christmas decorations weren't up yet, but the shopping season was already in full swing. The kids easily became lost in the shuffle as they walked in and out of the shops. Around five-thirty, Michelle received a call from her mom, asking where she was and what she wanted for dinner.

"I'm with Corey, Tim, and Paula," she replied. "How about pizza for all of us?"

"How about that sounds good," Marybelle said. "Where are you now?"

"Downtown on the square. Can you pick us up?"

Marybelle agreed and Michelle texted the others to meet outside Storm's Drugs. They ordered and picked up the pizzas on the way to the Pritchards.

After helping clean up from dinner, Michelle booted up her computer to catch up on email and other stuff. There was one addressed to both her and Corey.

To: mpritch35@email.com; coreypalm41@wordnet.com;
From: JedH@Hempleysboats.com

Dear kids,

I talked to my dad again, and he's agreed to talk to you. He didn't like your nosing around our place, but I told him I'd checked with the sheriff who said you're okay.

If you come out to our old farm tomorrow around 3:00 in the afternoon, Dad should be there. He said he'll explain about that tag and the boat you found at the bottom of the lake.

Sorry for the confusion earlier.

Jed Hempley

Michelle's phone rang as she read the message.

"Did you see the email from Mr. Hempley?" Corey asked.

"Uh-huh," Michelle said. "What do you want to do?"

"Let's go talk to him," Corey replied. "We might actually get answers."

"I'm not sure, Corey. We don't know either of the Hempleys very well. We need to be careful."

"We will, Shel. We'll take our phones and I'll let my mom know we're checking out a lead on the ring. You can tell your folks the same thing."

They agreed to meet at two o'clock Saturday then ride out to the Hempley farm.

Annette and Marybelle didn't object, provided both kids finished all their usual weekend chores first, and took their phones.

Later that night, an accident on the Interstate brought out most on-duty emergency personnel. Tyler Graves covered for the medical examiner's office. He didn't request assistance as there were no fatalities on the scene and he could process an accident on his own. As he finished up, he got a call from a sheriff's deputy. One of the victims died in the emergency room, so an autopsy would be needed. He called Dr. Driscoll.

"Sorry about this, boss," he said. "But we've got a body. Head-on crash with one fatality so far."

"That's okay," Driscoll replied. "I can come back tonight and do the exam tomorrow. Who's on then?"

"Paulie, I think," Graves said. "Should I let him know?"

"Yes, and then get all the samples."

"Blood, hair, saliva, nose swab, and tissue," Graves said. "Anything else?"

"That should do it, Tyler, thanks."

Dr. Driscoll got to her office by eight as usual. It might be Saturday, but there was work to do. Paulie was waiting for her. He had the body on the table and all the usual tools arranged for quick access.

"Good thing I get my coffee on the way in," she told her assistant.

"I figured you'd want to get it over with so you could still have part of the weekend."

"Don't worry about it. I can get caught up on paperwork while I'm here."

The exam went quickly with no unexpected issues. Cause of death was officially blunt-force trauma to the head. The victim's skull caved when he struck the steering wheel. After completing the job, Driscoll tossed her gloves into the waste bin and stripped off her surgical gown. Paulie labeled the samples and finished his forms. There was nothing left but wait for the toxicology and other reports to come back.

At her desk, Driscoll went through the mail from both yesterday and today. At the bottom was the report from the upstate lab. When the state crime lab couldn't provide more details, Driscoll sent tissue and other samples from the body in the lake there, looking for additional information and maybe a DNA match. The lab had access to different databases than the state.

She opened the envelope and began reading the report. When she came to the DNA results, she dropped the file back on the desk.

"No way!" she said out loud. "This is not possible!"

The report stated the DNA she'd sent was a familial match to someone in the National Law Enforcement Personnel Database. It listed the person, and Driscoll knew what her next step had to be.

The dead man was directly linked to someone she knew very well.

***

Corey rode over to Michelle's house at two o'clock.

"Ready?" he asked.

"Let's go," she said.

They headed out of town, making sure to stay well to the right on the roads. About a mile outside the city limits, they turned west on County Road 12. Hempley's farm was several more miles outside of Craigsville, down a dirt road marked by a mailbox. Riding down the road was easy, as the ruts were worn smooth from years of cars, trucks, and tractors going in and out.

At the end of the road, they came to the fenced main yard. Corey and Michelle chained their bikes to the fence rail and walked up to the quiet farmhouse. The door was slightly open, but no sound came from within.

"Are you sure this is where Mr. Hempley said to meet?" Michelle asked.

"I'm sure," Corey replied. "You got the same email."

"I know, but I don't like this. It's scary."

"You're right. But let's check it out."

"I'm going to call someone," Michelle said.

She took out her phone as Corey pushed the door open and they walked in. Michelle scrolled through her contacts for a number. As she did, the door slammed behind them.

They turned around to see Willie Hempley pointing a shotgun.

"Why can't you two mind your own business and leave well enough alone?" Hempley said. "There are just things best left hidden. Why'd you have to bring all this old stuff back up?"

Brenda Shelton cruised her patrol area out near the town's edge. Nothing out of sorts happening, but that's what the police did. Sometimes their presence kept things quiet. She listened to the radio, ready to respond to whatever came up when her cell rang. Following protocol, Shelton pulled to the side of the road and stopped. She looked at the caller ID and saw Michelle's name.

Now what does Michelle want? Shelton thought as she connected. Raising the phone to speak, she heard conversation.

"…leave well enough alone. There are just things best left hidden. Why'd you have to bring all this old stuff back up?"

"We haven't hurt anyone, sir," Shelton heard Michelle say. "We were just trying to find out who owned an old ring we found."

"We just wanted to solve a mystery," Corey added.

"Well this one shouldn't be," the man said. "And you've gotten into something you should've left alone."

Oh my lord, Shelton thought, *those kids are in trouble.*

"And now I've got to do something about it," the man's voice added.

Shelton muted her phone so she wouldn't be heard by the man and picked up her radio mike.

"Dispatch, this is patrol five."

"Go ahead."

"I've got an open call on my cell from Michelle Pritchard's phone. Can our system trace it and get me a location? I think the girl's in trouble, along with her friend, Corey."

"I don't know, but if not, I can contact the phone company. It may take a few minutes."

"Please hurry."

Sheriff Wingate was patrolling farther out in the county. He did patrol shifts occasionally, filling in for deputies needing time off if needed, though other times he did it to stay fresh and get out from behind his desk. Not that riding in a patrol unit was much different, but it helped him keep his procedures sharp.

He heard Shelton's conversation with dispatch as he cruised down County Road 12 west of Craigsville.

"Dispatch, this is county one," he radioed. "What this about tracing a call?"

"I have a request from city patrol five to trace," the dispatcher replied, "possibly someone in distress."

"Can you patch me through?"

"Wait one, Sheriff."

In seconds, Wingate was connected to Shelton. She quickly filled him in.

"It's the Palmer and Pritchard kids, Sheriff," she said. "I'm listening to a conversation, and I think they are in some kind of danger."

"Do you know who they are with?" Wingate asked.

"No, sir, that's why I asked for the trace," She paused to listen more.

"Honest," she heard Corey say, "we just wanted to learn about a man. Who he really was and where he came from."

"We were just trying to find out all we could about Paul Strickland," Michelle said, "or whoever he was."

"And why he ended up in Lake Cyrus," Corey said.

"I don't know who that is, boy, but it's none of your concern," the man said. "Though you seem bound and determined to find out, and I can't allow that."

"Please, Mr. Hempley," Wingate heard Michelle say, almost in tears. "We haven't done anything to hurt you."

Yes! Shelton thought. She picked up her mike.

"I've got him, Sheriff," she said. "It's Willie Hempley. I'll bet the kids are out at his place. I'm rolling now."

Wingate knew the man Shelton mentioned, and the place. He pulled back onto the road in the opposite direction. He'd passed the turn for Willie Hempley's farm a few miles back.

"That's county jurisdiction," he told Shelton. "I'm on it."

"But sir," Shelton replied, "this is Corey and Michelle. Whatever trouble they're in, I'm partly responsible. They've been helping me."

"Alright," Wingate replied, "but approach quietly. And follow my instructions."

"Yes, sir."

The sheriff retraced his route and turned down the unnamed road to Hempley's farm. As he parked next to the gated fence, he saw two bikes chained to it.

"Dispatch, this is county one," he radioed.

"I'm sorry, Sheriff," the dispatcher replied. "We haven't finished tracing that call."

"That's okay, I found them. City patrol five is also on the way, but send another back-up to Willie Hempley's place. Tell them to approach silently. No sirens."

"Yes, sir."

Wingate quietly got out of his car, drew his weapon, and walked up to the closed farmhouse door. He could hear voices from inside.

"No, I won't tell you the whole story," Willie Hempley said. "It's best left unheard, and wouldn't do you any good." He raised the weapon, aiming at the kids.

Sheriff Wingate turned the knob and pushed the door open.

"Put the gun down, Willie," he said entering the room. "I don't want to shoot you, but I can't let you hurt those kids."

Hempley didn't take his eyes from Corey and Michelle. "You ought to let me go ahead, Sheriff. This affects you too."

"It doesn't work that way," Wingate said. "And I'm not going to tell you again. Put the gun down *NOW!*"

Hempley slowly placed the gun on the floor. When he no longer had contact, the sheriff holstered his own weapon and handcuffed the other man.

"Are you kids alright?" he asked.

"Y-y-y-yessir," Michelle stammered. "He-he didn't hurt us."

"Good," the sheriff said. "I'll need to know all the details." He led Hempley outside.

"Right now, though, let's get back to town."

Brenda Shelton pulled up as the group walked down the steps. She got out and walked up.

"Is everything alright, Sheriff?" she asked.

"Everything's fine."

A sheriff's car arrived, and Wingate placed Hempley into that vehicle's back seat.

"Book him on assault with intent for now," he told the deputy. "Get him processed and into a cell. I'll talk to him later."

"You said you felt responsible," Wingate said to Shelton as the other car left, "and you probably are. But knowing these two, they'd have gotten deep into things anyway. Right now, though, we need to get this figured out. Meet me back at the office."

"Yes, sir!" Shelton said, turning back to her vehicle.

Wingate turned to Corey and Michelle, "Get in, kids, I need you in the office too."

"We've got our bikes, sir," Corey said.

"I don't care," Wingate said. "We need to wrap this up as soon as possible and I need your statements."

"But sir," Michelle said, "whenever you finish with us will be too late to come back and get them."

"Alright, alright," Wingate said, "here's what we'll do. Give me the keys or combinations and I'll send someone out here to get your bikes.

"Now get in the car."

"Ms. Pritchard," the sheriff continued as the kids began walking toward the car. "That was very smart and brave to call Officer Shelton. Nice job."

Michelle stopped. "Uh, thanks, sir. I guess," she said quietly. "But I was really trying to call my mom. I just got her by mistake."

Wingate laughed and got into the car.

Chapter XVII

Rich Geltsin leaned against the door as Sheriff Wingate and the others walked up.

"What are you doing here, Geltsin?" the sheriff asked.

"Chasing a story," the editor said, "I hear you have Willie Hempley in custody for something. What's going on?"

"None of your business," Wingate said. "Now get out of here."

"Oh, come on, Abe," Geltsin said, standing straight. "Do you really want to play it this way? You know darned well whatever's happening, I'll have the whole story from these two five minutes after you finish up with them." He gestured at Corey and Michelle.

"I can make sure they don't talk to you without permission," the sheriff said.

"I doubt that," Geltsin said. "Setting aside the First Amendment and all, look how successful you've been in the past telling them what to do."

Officer Shelton chuckled.

"But if you let me in on the whole thing now," he continued, "you'll be sure I get it right."

Wingate walked into the building.

"You're impossible, Geltsin," Shelton said as they all followed the sheriff.

"Not me, sister, just my constitutional prerogatives," he said.

"By the way," Shelton asked, "how'd you find out about this so quickly? We came straight from the scene, and I'll bet they haven't finished the processing."

"Did I ever tell you about my old reliable scanner?" Geltsin replied.

"You heard the call?" Shelton asked.

"Heard the whole thing," the editor said. "Started paying attention when you mentioned the kids. Figured it'd be interesting, so I came right over."

"Which detective is on call?" the sheriff asked Sergeant DuPree as the group passed the front desk.

"Harding," DuPree answered.

"Get him in here."

"Hey, Sheriff," Geltsin called out, "That reminds me. Mo Driscoll dropped something off for the detectives while I was waiting. Wouldn't tell me what."

"At least someone knows how to follow the rules," Wingate said as he went to his office.

"Alright, listen up," the sheriff said. "Officer Shelton, go check on where they are with the processing. When they're finished back there, have the man taken to interrogation."

"You two," he continued, pointing to Corey and Michelle. "I'll need a full statement from you. I know you were together, so you don't have give me separate ones. Work on it while I get my notes in order, then you can watch from the observation room."

"What about me?" the editor asked.

"You can watch the questioning too," Wingate answered, "but no recording. And if he asks for his lawyer, you all have to leave."

It took another ten minutes before Officer Shelton came back. Willie Hempley was booked and waiting in the interrogation room. Corey, Michelle, and Rich Geltsin followed Shelton to the observation room as the sheriff headed into interrogation with his case files. On the way, he told Sergeant DuPree to have Detective Harding join when he arrived.

"Alright, Willie," Sheriff Wingate said, taking the seat opposite. "Let's do this right. You don't have to say anything to me if you don't want to. You have the right to remain silent..."

"I know my rights, Abe," Hempley said. "Let's just get on with this."

"I still have to do this," Wingate said. "As I was saying; you have the right to an attorney and one will be provided if you can't afford one."

"I don't need a lawyer."

"So you're waiving your rights?"

"Yeah, yeah, whatever. I just want to know what you're gonna do about those two brats. What right do they have poking around my business?"

Wingate opened the file in front of him. "Look, Willie, no matter what those kids did, you can't go around threatening to shoot them. And it seems you lured them out to your farm with an email suggesting you'd tell them what they wanted to know."

"That was my boy's dumb idea. He thought those kids would leave me alone if I just told them about that tag and that old boat. But they were after more than that, weren't they?"

"Willie, those kids found the body and your old boat down in the lake. They just wanted to know who he was and how he got there."

"Well, that and who owned the ring I found," Corey said quietly in the observation room.

"And the trail simply led to you and your boats," Wingate continued. "They were just asking questions."

"They don't have the right," Hempley said loudly. "They're nosy little brats who need to be taken care of."

"That's not your call," Wingate said. "Besides, now I'm interested, and I do have the right. So why don't you start telling me what this is all about. What's so secret you need to threaten two thirteen-year-olds with a shotgun?"

"Let me ask you something, Sheriff," Hempley said. "What do you really know about your mama and daddy?"

"What do Mort and Clara have to do with this?"

"Just about everything," Hempley replied. "I hate being the one to tell you after all these years, but old Mort Wingate isn't really your daddy."

Wingate stared at his prisoner for several seconds.

"That's right, Sheriff," Hempley said. "Your daddy ain't your daddy."

"Willie, you'll have to do better," he said. "That isn't exactly news. Just about everyone in this county knows I'm adopted.

"Lord, I've known since I was twelve."

"But did you ever know who your real daddy was?" Hempley asked. Wingate shook his head.

"Well, you do now, boy," Hempley continued. "Your real daddy was Pete Simpkins, the man those kids found in the lake."

Wingate never knew who his biological parents were, mostly because he'd never asked. Mort and Clara told him the truth after schoolmates harassed him about it in grade school. As far as Abe Wingate cared, the Wingates were his folks.

Bobby Harding walked into observation with the file Dr. Driscoll delivered earlier.

"I have to talk with the sheriff before this goes further."

"What have you got, Detective?" Officer Shelton asked.

"New information on the dead man from the medical examiner."

He gave the file to Shelton who quickly skimmed it.

"My god," she said, handing the file back. She rapped on the glass to get Wingate's attention.

Wingate closed his files and left interrogation. In the hall, he walked up to Harding and Shelton.

"What's this about?"

"You need to see this, Sheriff," Detective Harding said. "It's pretty conclusive and changes everything."

Wingate read the report summary.

"This doesn't change anything, Bobby," he said. "It just confirms what Willie just told me. It doesn't tell us why Simpkins was killed or how he ended up in the lake."

"Yeah, but now we've got some leverage," Harding replied. "Now we can see where it leads."

Harding and Wingate went back into interrogation.

"Looks like you're telling the truth, Willie," Harding said as the two men sat.

"But so what?" Sheriff Wingate said. "So what if Pete Simpkins was my real father. He's long dead and my parents raised me."

"Because it's only part of the story," Hempley replied. "The rest is who your real mama is and then how Simpkins ended up in the lake."

"I'm listening," Wingate said.

"Do you know who your real mama is?"

"I never asked."

"Well, here's the shocker for you, Sheriff," Hempley said. "Your mama really *is* your mama."

Behind the glass in the observation room, Corey's eyes grew wide and Michelle gasped.

Brenda Shelton muttered, "Oh my lord in heaven."

"What in hell are you talking about?" Wingate said.

"You really don't know, do you, Abe?" Hempley said. The sheriff stared at him.

"Okay, here it is. Your folks, Mort and Clara, went steady through high school. Most people figured they'd get married afterward, but things worked out a little bit differently."

"What's this have to do with the dead man?" Detective Harding asked.

"Just setting the timeline," Hempley answered. "Anyway, they both started college, but could only afford to go part-time. Then Mort got his draft notice. This was the late sixties, remember, and he decided to enlist in the Marines instead."

"He asked Clara to marry him right before he left for basic," Hempley continued, "and things went on."

"When did Simpkins show up?" Wingate asked.

"And what about you?" Harding added. "Why weren't you drafted?"

"My number didn't come up," Hempley said. "And it's not important."

"Anyway, Pete Simpkins wandered in one day in late sixty-nine. He said he'd just gotten out of the Navy and was hitch-hiking and working his way home while he decided what to do with his life. He was looking for a job, and my dad and I needed some help with the farm and the boat shop. So we hired him. Gave him a room out at the lake too."

"Did he cause trouble for you?" Harding asked.

"Not on the job," Hempley said. "He was a decent worker, but he liked playing around more. He spent most of his off-time drinking, hustling pool, and picking fights. He was real good at all three."

"Not that good," Wingate said. "We know he was arrested several times."

"Yeah, but that was minor stuff," Hempley continued. "Simpkins also liked the ladies and was always trying to get them to put out. That's what got him into trouble."

"What happened?" Harding asked.

"He tried to pick up Clara one night out at the old joint by the mill. She didn't want anything to do with him, but Pete sort of insisted. However it happened—and I wasn't there—she ended up leaving with him.

"The next morning, she staggers into the hospital, beaten and cut, and saying she was raped. Old Doc Frobisher checked her out and reported that she'd been assaulted. The sheriff got her to swear out a complaint and they arrested Pete."

"Was he convicted?" Harding asked.

"Nope," Hempley said. "It went to trial, and the prosecutor had a pretty good case. But back then there wasn't much science, so all he had was her statements and the doctor's report."

"Thing was," he went on, "Simpkins' lawyer turned it all around when he questioned Clara. By the time he was done, she was in tears and the jury was convinced she'd brought it on herself, that she'd asked for it."

"I don't believe this," Officer Shelton said angrily to the others in the observation room.

"Believe it," Rich Geltsin said. "It's still a tried and true defense in rape cases."

"It's still wrong," Michelle said. Corey nodded.

"Is that it?" Wingate asked.

"Hell no," Hempley said, "it's just getting started."

"A couple of months after the trial, Clara finds out she's pregnant. Abortion wasn't legal back then, so there aren't many options. She decides to leave, says something about needing to *find herself,* but most people knew. She comes back a few months later."

"When did Mort come back?" Harding asked.

"A few weeks after Clara came home," Hempley said. "I don't know what happened, but she wanted to break off the engagement. Mort really loved her, though, and wouldn't hear it."

"Did she tell him what happened?"

"She must have, though he'd have found out anyway. It was public knowledge."

"Anyway," Hempley continued, "That's when it really got bad. Mort, Clara, me and another girl were out one evening when Pete showed up. It was not good..."

"Well, looky here," Pete Simpkins said, walking up to where the four friends sat. "I believe Miss Clara has found her a new play toy. You branching out now, honey?"

"Shut up, jackass," Mort said, "and go away."

"Don't be that way, boy," Simpkins said. "She's got plenty to go around. I ought to know."

Mort stood up and faced Pete. "Watch your mouth or I'll close it permanently."

Simpkins laughed. "You could try, faggot, but I could break you in half, screw your girl silly again, and still make it work bright-eyed and bushy-tailed. Ain't I right, Willie?"

Willie Hempley tried to settle things down. "Maybe that's what you should think about, Pete. We've got a lot to do out at the lake tomorrow, so why don't you head home so we can get an early start."

By this time, the bartender saw what was happening and came over.

"That's a good idea, Simpkins," he said. "Why don't you get on out of here and go home. At least take your business somewhere else."

"Simpkins left, and so did we a little while later," Hempley said. "After dropping the girls at their homes, Mort and I split up. I went home, but couldn't sleep. I was worried Mort would try something. He was as mad as I'd ever seen. I also figured I should check on whether Simpkins actually went back to his room, so I drove up to the lake.

"But I was too late. When I got there, I found Mort out at the end of the dock, wrapping a chain around something. I ran out to see what happened…"

"What the hell's going on?" Willie asked.

"I did it, Willie," Mort said, "I took care of the bastard."

"What do you mean?"

"I killed him. I came up here to have it out with him. I told him I knew what he'd done to Clara and even though he got away with it in court, he wasn't getting away with it from me."

"So what happened?"

"The asshole just laughed. He said he'd do it again if he got the chance. Said I'd be glad he was around because Clara needed a REAL man. That's when I went after him. We fought and I grabbed a pipe and bashed his head. I think I caved his skull in."

"We have to call the police, Mort," Willie said. "We can tell them about the fight, and it will be self-defense."

"Like hell," Mort answered. "I'm not gonna put Clara through this again. Besides, nobody's gonna miss this idiot.

"Now either help me or get lost."

"Okay, I'll help."

"I asked Mort what he wanted to do with the body, and he said he wanted to bolt the chain to the bottom of one of our rowboats and then sink it out in the middle of the lake. The problem was these newer boats really wouldn't sink. They were so light, you could cut a hole in the bottom and the thing might settle just below the surface but not really sink."

"So what did you do?" Harding asked.

"We loaded the boat with Simpkins' body full of dirt, sand, rocks and gravel," Hempley said. "Almost enough to sink it. Then we took another boat and towed it out to a deep part of the lake. When we got out there, we tossed in another couple hundred pounds of stuff and down she went. I figured the pressure down deep would keep the thing on the bottom."

"And I was right, too," Hempley continued. "Until those two dumbass kids found it and started asking questions."

"Willie," Wingate said, "someone would have found the body anyway after the lake was drained."

"Yeah, but nobody would have cared."

"Is that the whole story?" Harding asked.

"Nope. After we sunk the boat, we each swore we'd never say a word to anyone about it. Didn't either, until now."

"What about you reporting two stolen boats?"

"That was Mort's idea. He said it'd be good misdirection and would point any suspicion away from me."

"Anything else, Willie?"

"Well, Mort and Clara got married the next spring. But then they found Clara couldn't have any more kids. Apparently the rape and a hard delivery messed her up inside. So, a few months later, they went off and adopted you from somewhere."

The room was silent for several seconds, then Sheriff Wingate stood up and stacked his files.

"That's enough," he said. "Finish up, Bobby. Get a full written statement and put him back in his cell." He turned to the glass separating interrogation from the observation room.

"Go home, everyone. We're finished."

In the hall, the others stopped the sheriff as he came out of interrogation.

"What's next?" Officer Shelton asked.

"That's not up to me," Wingate answered. "We'll put everything together and send it to the prosecutor's office. They can deal with it now."

"I've got a few more questions," Rich Geltsin said.

"Too bad," Wingate replied. "I don't have any more answers." He walked toward his office.

"Wow," Corey said, "this is really crazy. I never dreamed there was so much involved."

"Me neither," Michelle said, "and it wasn't even the guy we were looking for."

"But you found him," Shelton said.

"And it's not over yet," Geltsin said. "This is going to be one heckuva story, and I need to get busy."

"Can we help?" Corey asked.

"Not tonight," Shelton said. "We need to get you two home before your parents start another county-wide search."

Rich Geltsin headed to the paper's old downtown office. He booted up a workstation and compiled his notes into a working order, then began writing a basic outline. He worked until about four in the morning when he couldn't focus on the screen anymore. He saved his efforts, went home to grab a few hours sleep, and was back at the paper's main office Sunday afternoon to set Monday's edition. The story would take several more days to finish.

Officer Shelton delivered the kids safely home, explaining to Mrs. Palmer and the Pritchards why Corey and Michelle were so late. There almost was a search, but when Annette called the sheriff's office, Sergeant DuPree told her the kids were safe, but involved in an active investigation.

"You had better have a really good explanation, Corey," Annette told her son.

"I know, Mom," Corey said. "And I'm pretty sure I do. But can it wait until tomorrow? I'm beat."

"Then go to bed."

Sheriff Wingate dumped his files and notes onto his desk and sat down. He reached into a drawer and pulled out a glass and a bottle of well-aged bourbon. He poured a large helping and drank it down.

Then he poured another, and another. As he finished his fourth glass, there was a knock on the doorframe.

"You alright, Abe?" Chief Blaise asked. "You want some company?"

"No."

"You sure look like you could use some," the chief said, taking the chair across the desk from Wingate.

"Brenda Shelton filled me in on everything," Blaise continued. "and I just wanted to see if you wanted to talk about it."

"I'd rather drink," Wingate said.

"Okay, so pour me one and we'll do both."

"Robert," Wingate said, after filling a second glass and passing it over, "have you ever had everything you believed in and thought was true ripped out from under you and turned upside down?

"Not since Cheryl left me," Blaise said. "Why don't you lay it out?"

Two hours and the rest of the bottle gave Chief Blaise the story. When they finished, the chief asked Sergeant DuPree to have any available officer or deputy come in from patrol to take the men home.

Chapter XVIII

"So now you're *special correspondents?*" Ron Isaacs said as he projected the morning's *Record / Times* front page on the screen. Corey and Michelle said nothing as several students in the class chuckled.

"It's a great story, you two," Isaacs continued. "And I can't wait for the rest of it."

Rich Geltsin wrote a three-part series of stories about the body in the lake, producing them under his by-line with help from *Corey Palmer & Michelle Pritchard, Record / Times Special Correspondents.* The first appeared two Mondays after Willie Hempley's arrest, highlighting how the kids found the body and describing the medical examiner's initial findings.

Today's story detailed how Corey and Michelle found out about Pete Simpkins while trying to find the owner of the old ring. The story also told about how the face was reconstructed and ended with the incident at Hempley's farm and the arrest. Next Monday's story would wrap things up with Hempley's statement and Sheriff Wingate's family history. Paul Strickland and the ring ended up being part of both the later installments,

Wingate approved Geltsin's writing about his parentage. Mort and Clara passed away in the early nineties, so no one would be harmed. The sheriff didn't like it, but realized he couldn't do much about it. So he went along. In return, Geltsin interviewed him at length for a complete picture of his folks.

Corey and Michelle took gentle ribbing throughout the day. Their friends wanted details, and kids they didn't know well wanted to talk and give them a little grief.

The story even impressed Tommy Cooper and his friends. During one break that morning, he intentionally bumped into Corey in the hallway and Joey Halston did the same to Michelle.

"Nice job out there, Palmer," Tommy said as he made contact. "Looks like you've got guts after all."

"You too, girl," Joey said to Michelle. "No one's gonna mess with you."

Corey clenched his fist and took a step after the others, but Tim held him back.

"Don't do it, man," Tim said. "It's not worth it."

"Tim's right," Paula added. "Besides, that's probably the closest thing to a compliment you'll ever get from those guys."

The county prosecutor declined to bring charges against Willie Hempley beyond his threatening Corey and Michelle. There just wasn't enough evidence, he told Judge Danielson. Hempley pled guilty and was sentenced to six months in jail.

The story held Craigsville's attention for another few weeks until the holidays changed everyone's focus. By the time the New Year rolled around, life was settling back into a more usual routine.

Brenda Shelton got an unexpected gift of well-earned sergeant's stripes effective on January 1st.

At school, the semester wound down with final exams. Corey and Michelle once again faced coming up with a research project for spring as Mr. Isaacs wouldn't let them use their work on the dead body or the old ring.

"It wouldn't be fair to everyone else," he told them, "since all your work is already done. Besides, everyone knows how it comes out."

Three weeks into January, a smartly dressed Navy lieutenant walked into Danielson's office and asked to see the judge. Annette asked him what it was about.

"A request the judge made several months ago," the Lieutenant said.

He introduced himself as Lieutenant Greg Hearell from the Defense Personnel Archives in St. Louis.

"Why would you be here, Lieutenant?" Danielson asked.

"Sir, several months ago, you requested information on a nineteen sixty-five graduate from the Naval Academy through the alumni foundation."

"That's correct," Danielson said. "Two young people found a class ring and wanted to learn who it belonged to."

"Yes, sir," Hearell said. "A Lieutenant Paul Malcolm Strickland. I'm here to confirm the lieutenant's identity and to take possession of the body so it can be properly buried. I'm also here for the ring so it can be returned to his family."

"The file we saw said Strickland didn't have family," Annette said.

"That's not quite true, ma'am," Hearell said. "The academy wouldn't necessarily know about any extended family. However, Lieutenant Strickland did have a sister and today her grandson is serving in the Marines. We have his DNA profile, and should be able to determine a familial match."

"So you'd like to do DNA testing on the remains?" Danielson asked.

"If needed," Hearell said, "but I understand you've done substantial testing on the remains, so that may not be necessary."

"Alright," Danielson said, "I can have the medical examiner provide you with all her reports and release the remains to you. But you should know, young man, there's more to the story."

"How so, sir?"

"For starters, your Lieutenant Strickland was known as Pete Simpkins here in Wagner County, and he had a rather checkered history."

"And there's the story of how he was found," Annette added.

Judge Danielson scribbled a note and handed it to Annette.

"Go pick up Corey and Michelle," he said. "This will get them released early. I'll call Dr. Driscoll and Sheriff Wingate. We'll get together in the conference room."

"What about Sergeant Shelton?" Annette asked. "She uncovered a lot of the information."

"I'll round her up too," Danielson said. "And I think I'll call Rich Geltsin, also. He'll never let us hear the end if we leave him out of the story."

Much to Mrs. Hollis's dismay, Corey left English class after being summoned to the principal's office. He was a little confused, but when Annette explained why, he got excited.

Michelle left her math class completely bewildered. Why would Mrs. Palmer need her, she wondered. Like Corey, she became excited when Annette explained what was going on.

Everyone gathered in the conference room by ten-thirty. Ten people crowded the room somewhat, but there were enough seats at the large table. Judge Danielson sat at one end, with the Lieutenant at the other. Maureen Driscoll brought copies of all her reports to pass along.

Judge Barker joined the group, along with Chief Blaise. Danielson introduced Lieutenant Hearell to the others and asked him to start things off.

"I mean no offense, Your Honor," Hearell said, "but my information isn't intended for publication. I'm not comfortable discussing this with a reporter present."

"I'm not offended," Geltsin said, "but I'm not leaving either."

"This is the way it works, Lieutenant," Danielson said, "This story is already very public here in Wagner County, and Mr. Geltsin isn't just entitled to whatever information you have, he was invited."

"Besides," Sheriff Wingate muttered, "he'd have the whole story five minutes after we're done anyway." Geltsin and Sergeant Shelton heard this and tried hard not to laugh.

"Very well," Hearell said, removing a file from his briefcase. "I wish I could tell you I'm here to claim the remains of a hero so they can be interred with appropriate honors. Sadly, though, that is not the case."

Hearell opened the file. "Paul Malcolm Strickland was born and raised in Washington State. He entered the U.S. Naval Academy in the fall of nineteen sixty-one and graduated with his class four years later. His final ranking was two hundred and third out of four hundred sixty. While his academic record was above average, he accumulated several hundred demerits and had a number of disciplinary incidents."

"Fighting and the like, I'd bet," Judge Barker said.

"That's true," Lieutenant Hearell said. "Strickland seemed to create havoc on many occasions."

"After graduation, Ensign Strickland underwent flight training in Galveston and Pensacola, receiving his wings in July of nineteen sixty-six. He then trained on the F-4 Phantom and was assigned first to the USS Independence and then the USS Enterprise. He was promoted to lieutenant (j.g.) on schedule."

"Was he still getting into trouble?" Geltsin asked.

"There were several incidents requiring disciplinary action noted," Hearell said. "Most involving fighting or disorderly conduct while on shore leave."

"During his second deployment to Vietnam with VF 116," Hearell continued, "Lieutenant Strickland was returning from a mission over the DMZ and was shot down. His squadron leader reported seeing Strickland's plane descend into the trees, but no resulting explosion. This was March of nineteen sixty-nine."

"And nothing was ever found?" Judge Danielson asked. "No wreckage or body?"

"No, sir," Hearell answered. "He was listed as missing in action. After the cease-fire and release of the prisoners in seventy-three, his record was updated to be presumed dead."

"And then he shows up here," Sheriff Wingate said.

"As Pete Simpkins, and ends up at the bottom of Lake Cyrus where our two young friends found him last fall," Chief Blaise added.

"That's when we found the ring, too," Corey said.

"How did you put it all together?" Lieutenant Hearell asked.

"Some luck and a lot of persistence," Chief Blaise said.

For the next half-hour, everyone told the lieutenant how the remains were tested, researched, and questioned.

"Since the body was in the lake for so long," Sergeant Shelton said during the discussion, "we started with old newspapers. We were looking for someone reported missing who matched the description from back then."

"How did you know the ring was connected to the body?" Hearell asked.

"We didn't at first," Corey said. "We were just trying to find out who it belonged to after we found the initials inside."

"We checked old high school yearbooks and lists of graduating classes for someone with those initials who was going to the Naval Academy," Michelle said.

"We didn't find anyone matching the initials," Corey said, "But did find Pete Simpkins and all his arrests."

"We also found the stories about his arrest and trial for rape," Michelle said.

"It was later when we connected things," Corey said.

"That's well and good," Lieutenant Hearell said, "but I'm here to confirm the remains are Paul Strickland."

"It's all part of the story, son," Judge Barker said.

Dr. Driscoll opened her laptop and passed copies of her records over to Hearell.

"If you have your DNA profile on a flash drive, I can run the comparison with ours," she said.

"Sorry, all I have are paper copies," he replied.

"That's alright," Driscoll said, opening another folder. "I've got mine on transparency. We can do this the old-fashioned way."

Dr. Driscoll laid her DNA profile over Lieutenant Hearell's document, making notes on where things aligned and didn't. Then she did the same with Sheriff Wingate's, making similar notes.

"We have the correct familial markers," she said. "And if I were called to testify, I would state these exemplars are indeed from related men."

"Who is the other person you compared Strickland's DNA to?" Hearell asked.

"His biological son," Sheriff Wingate said. "Me."

"Oh," Hearell said, "That complicates matters. As the closest living relation, you have priority on claiming the remains."

"I'll sign any release you want," Wingate said. "I don't want anything to do with him."

Hearell removed a form from his briefcase and passed in to Sheriff Wingate.

"Now there's the matter of the ring," he said.

Corey reached into his pocket. "It's right here. I've been carrying it as sort of a good luck charm." He passed it to the lieutenant.

"Very good," Hearell said.

"What happens now?" Michelle asked.

"Well, unless there's a reason to keep Strickland's remains here, they will be transported to wherever his family desires and interred there."

Judge Danielson looked around the table for reactions.

"I don't think that's going to be a problem," he said. "I think we'll all be glad to see the last of this gentleman, and close the books on another mystery."

Everyone at the table nodded.

Corey turned to Michelle and smiled. She gave him one in return and held out her fist. He bumped it and winked.

***

Corey and Michelle made it back to school for lunch and they told their friends about the meeting at the courthouse.

"So you didn't really learn anything new," Tim said.

"Not really," Michelle said, "Just that the man we found had a history we didn't know."

"And that he was trouble for a long time," Corey said.

"But the lieutenant took the body?" Paula asked.

"He will," Michelle said, "At least that's what he said."

"We had to give the ring back, too," Corey added.

Tommy Cooper turned from the next table.

"So you're finally done with finding bodies, huh?"

"Don't start, Cooper," Corey said.

"Hey! I'm just asking, Palmer," Tommy said, coming over to where the others sat. "Don't be a jerk."

"He's not," Michelle said, "But you are."

"Shut up, you little…"

"Easy, man," Mike Bates cut in. "You know how she can get."

"I just wanted to know whose body you're gonna look for next," Tommy said.

"We haven't decided yet, have we, Corey?" Michelle said.

"Nope," Corey said, "You volunteering, Cooper?"

www.ingramcontent.com/pod-product-compliance
Lightning Source LLC
Chambersburg PA
CBHW030408180626
46812CB00005B/1966